BILLY BOBBLE

AND THE WITCH HUNT

Also by R.S. Mellette

Novel

Billy Bobble Makes a Magic Wand (2014)

Short stories in anthologies published by
Elephant's Bookshelf Press

"The Sound of the Chain"
in *Horrors: Real, Imagined, and Deadly* (2015)

"Children of the Trees" in *Summer's Edge* (2013)

"The Last Performance of the Neighborhood Summer
Theatre Festival" in *The Fall* (2012)

"The Idea Exchange" in *Spring Fevers* (2012)

BILLY BOBBLE

AND THE WITCH HUNT

BY R.S. MELLETTE

EBP

Billy Bobble and the Witch Hunt

Book Design: Matt Sinclair
Illustrator: Kirbi Fagan
Cover Design: Charlee Hoffman
Editor: Matt Sinclair

Elephant's Bookshelf Press, LLC
Springfield, N.J. 07081
www.elephantsbookshelfpress.com

ISBN-13: 978-1-940180-17-5
Printed in the United States of America.

For my Mom. Rest easy.

THE FIRST SPELL

THE COPS WERE COMING.

The learned doctor of physics, currently teaching high school science, had to work fast if he wanted to improve his professional status. The minute he'd witnessed Billy Bobble appear out of thin air in a locked police interrogation room, grab his friend Suzy Quinofski, and together disappear again, the professor knew what he was going to do, and that he'd have to work fast.

That was how many days ago? A week or two; and it was no magician's trick. There had been no curtains, no misdirection, and, as far as the kids knew, no audience. None, except himself, and he was the only person within a hundred miles who could have understood the monumental scientific achievement the two 12-year-olds had pulled off, and which he would soon take credit for accomplishing.

He knew the second he erased the surveillance video that he'd bought himself only a short amount of time, maybe days, maybe hours. In that time, he would have to talk his biology counterpart at Oakridge prep school into taking a DNA sample from him, separate the coding from non-coding portions — without breaking the chain, and without knowing why she was doing it. He would have to find a piece of wood he could work with, split it length-wise, put the separated DNA inside, wrap it with copper wire in the right way, so, when charged with a current, it would create a magnetic implosion field to push the DNA molecules into ... what? He didn't know for sure: a different quantum state of matter? A different dimension? He didn't have time to figure it out. Once he'd erased the tape, he'd committed a felony and put himself on a path that led to the inevitable — two police detectives strolling up his sidewalk.

The glue on his staff required twenty-four hours to set. His woodworking skills were nowhere near those of Billy's brother, Peter, so he'd chosen a five-foot-tall walk-ing stick instead of Billy's novelty wand. Only an hour ago he'd clamped the vise grips around what he hoped would be ... magic.

He had also hoped the police would take one more day to figure out what happened to their video tape, but he was wrong. Detectives Mark Danner and Alan Reins — the ones from Suzy's interrogation — were knocking at his door.

"Dr. Menaus," said one.

Menaus recognized the voice to be the senior partner, Detective Danner.

"Dr. Anton Menaus."

Time had run out.

Another knock. Then Reins said, "We know you're home, Doc. We just want to ask you a few questions."

Menaus concentrated on his task, unscrewing the vise grips. He had to be careful. He would only get one chance at this. One chance to do the thing he knew must be done first. Dr. Menaus, a man of science, had been planning a spell. The only kind of spell that could buy him the time he needed to set his life right, to give him the rewards and respect he knew he deserved.

"Anton," said Reins after another pounding at the door. "We know you erased the tape. We just want to talk to you about it."

Over the week he'd perfected his spell down to a single word. One word that would set him free and make him the sole proprietor of the most powerful tool ever created: magic.

"Dr. Menaus, we have a warrant. Don't make us break the door down."

He raised his staff, pressed the button with his thumb, and spoke the single word.

"Forget."

One

A Funny Thing Happened on the Way to School

"DO YOU KNOW WHY you're here, Billy?"

"What?"

"Haven't you been paying attention?"

"No, I haven't."

"Fine, we'll start again. My name is Dr. Cassandra Weston. I'm a psychiatrist. You're in the emergency room, of—"

Billy sighed. He knew who Dr. Weston was. She'd told him three times. He knew he was in the ER of Winston Memorial Hospital. He'd been there before.

"I remember your name, and I know where I am."

"Do you know why you're here?"

"Yeah," said Billy. Of course he knew. It was right on the tip of his mind. Then it wasn't. "Uh."

"Do you know how you got those injuries?"

If she hadn't mentioned it, Billy wouldn't have known he was injured, but now that she did, he realized his head was killing him. He had a bandage taped to his forehead, bruises up and down his arms, and the injured ribs on his left side made breathing difficult. "Did I get beat up again?"

"According to the police," said Dr. Weston. "You were the one doing the beating."

"That doesn't sound like me." Billy had been roughed up by bullies at school. It sort of came with the territory of being King of the Geeks. Not once had he ever struck back.

"You attacked a teacher."

Now Billy was really confused. School had only been out for a week. He had all of summer vacation ahead of him. And besides, he liked teachers. He told Dr. Weston as much.

"Not your teacher," she said. "Dr. Menaus, at Oakridge Academy."

Billy tried to keep his face from showing his shock. Dr. Weston took down a note, and Billy realized he hadn't been successful.

"You know, I went to Oakridge in high school," said Dr. Weston. "I had Dr. Menaus. I can think of several reasons why I might want to beat him up. But can you tell me why you did?"

"Don't you know? Didn't the police tell you?"

She adjusted her office-appropriate, but not-too-dowdy skirt as if she were trying to hide some uncertainty. "I want you to tell me."

"I must have gotten a pretty big bump on the head, because I don't remember a thing."

"Let's see if we can't prime the memory pump a little."

Billy got the impression she was quoting directly from a textbook she'd read not too long ago, which made him wonder. "Should I even be talking to you? My brother always tells me, when dealing with the cops, don't say a word without your attorney present."

"Sounds like he might have learned from some experience."

"Yeah, way too much."

"To answer your question, you can talk to me. My doctoral dissertation centered on initial criminal behavior. As part of my lab work, I provided psychiatric counselling to the Winston Police Department for first-time offenders, or those whose offenses were more like disturbances than actual crimes. The program was such a success that they let me stay on as a way for me to pay back my student loans. The next time we meet will be in my office at the police station."

"That means we have doctor-patient confidentiality?"

"Very good, Billy. Yes, it does. Anything you say to me will be held in confidence unless a person's life is at risk."

Billy considered that for a moment, then agreed.

Dr. Weston picked up where she left off. "You arrived on campus at Oakridge Academy…"

"Why was I there?"

"I was hoping you would tell me."

"I don't know," said Billy. "I mean, I used to go there all the time. Dr. Menaus would let me use the lab and borrow textbooks I couldn't get anywhere else, but ever since Suzy and I tried to blow up Winston High—"

"Wait, what?!" Dr. Weston had been reading her notes from the police report and nearly missed that last comment. "You tried to blow up the school?"

"Not really, but, that's got to be in my record, right?"

"It isn't. I know it's not." She spoke more to herself than to Billy. "I always check for any violent offenses prior to being alone with any patient, even a kid."

"Should you be telling me that?"

She didn't hear Billy's question as she was flipping through his file. "Billy, there is nothing here about you trying to blow up the school, or anything like that. Your file is the most impressive I've ever seen."

"Thank you."

She pulled out some blank paper. "Though someone seems to have used it to store printer paper." She tossed them aside and got back to Billy. "Why do you think you tried to blow up the school?"

It was Billy's turn to shift in his government-issued green pleather and gray steel chair. His memory of the whole thing was spotty. All he knew was he and Suzy got into a lot of trouble. "I don't know. We didn't, really — try to blow up the school, I mean. We were doing an experiment that went wrong."

"An experiment?"

"Yeah, you know, physics. That's my thing."

"Yes, I saw that, but… we'll talk about that later. Let's get back to what happened today. You were going to Oakridge…"

"I remember going to bed last night," said Billy. For some reason his recollection of the past twenty-four hours was like a jigsaw puzzle with pieces missing. "I remember getting up this morning. I remember the police bandaging my head and the nurse at Oakridge saying that I might have a concussion. Then the ambulance, waiting around here a lot, and now I'm talking to you."

"You mentioned Suzy before. Who is she?"

"Suzy is my best friend."

"Do you think she'll know why you attacked Professor Menaus?"

"YOU WANT TO TALK about it?"

Suzy was sympathetic. She could see Billy was hurting as much on the inside as the bruises showed on the outside. "What kind of trouble did you get into?"

Billy washed down his peanut butter and honey on a cracker with a swig of milk. "I have to see the psychiatrist once a week until she says otherwise." In truth, his talks with Suzy in the basement biology lab her parents set up to support her science habit always made him feel better. Billy thought a real best friend beat a hired one every time.

Case in point, Suzy's perfect response to Billy's predicament. "Oh, so public humiliation and exposure to adolescent ridicule. Whatever happened to the punishment fitting the crime?"

"It's only public humiliation if someone finds out."

"Don't look at me," said Suzy. "I'm not telling anyone."

"I know. Thanks." Suzy had earned her best-friend status over and over again in Billy's life. This would be just one more gold star.

"So, instead of public humiliation, you're living a lie, encouraged by the state. Nice."

And so went their summer. Suzy's Dad, a general in charge of Special Forces, had pulled off some crazy operation to save a bunch of captured soldiers as the previous school year ended. The aftermath of that action made the past few weeks seem like a blur.

"What do you want to do for our birthdays?" Suzy asked.

Billy and Suzy were born on the same day thirteen years earlier, and had been best friends for the past ten. They never really had big parties. With a mid-July birth date, most of the kids they knew were on vacation, so it was hard to gather a crowd big enough to warrant a party. At least, that's what Suzy let her mom think. She didn't want to broach the subject of her not having a lot of close friends besides Billy. Not that it bothered her. Suzy wasn't a big people person. Being the daughter of the most important general on the base meant her mom could fill the neighborhood with kids for a party if Suzy wanted it. They did that once.

According to the family mythology, when Suzy was three the Quinofskis threw a party for her, inviting nearly every kid in town her age. Suzy hated it. She refused to come out of her room the entire time. After the guests had left, Mrs. Quinofski found her and Billy reading *The Cat in the Hat* to each other. Since no one had really tried to teach either kid how to read, the event was seen as some sort of scholarly miracle. At least, that's the way the story was told at every birthday party since.

"What did we do last year?" asked Billy.

"Pretended like the idea of going to high school two years ahead of everyone else didn't scare us and studied in the library all day."

"I wasn't scared of going to high school."

"Yeah, right," said Suzy.

"Well, not the classes, anyway."

Suzy let the subject die, and a silence fell between them. That had been happening a lot lately. They both had heavy issues on their minds, like whether Billy was losing his or not. It was fine for them to joke about him going to therapy, but they didn't talk about his mother being schizophrenic, which meant he had a good chance of having the affliction as well.

They equally did not talk about their fathers. Billy's had been out of the picture since he was born. Until recently, Suzy's had been somewhere in the Middle East. Ever since one of his top secret missions from last spring, the world seemed to have lost its mind. Paramilitary groups were popping up everywhere doing horrible things to people for no apparent reason. General Quinofski was home now, but not his usual self. In fact, the whole world seemed to be in a bad mood.

And that wasn't all. "Did you see the news?" asked Suzy

"Now what?"

"They've formed a Federal School Board."

"So?"

"They want teachers all over the country to teach the

exact same thing to every kid in every state every day. They are pushing a federal daily curriculum."

"So?"

"They want to standardize all of the textbooks in the country."

"Who does?"

"Mom calls them, 'backwoods ignorant lunatics,' but the rest of the world calls them Congress."

"It'll never happen. Congress can't get anything done."

"I don't know. They've been talking about it a lot on TV."

"So what if they do?" asked Billy.

"If they change a lot, you might have to actually work for a living."

"What are you talking about?"

"You've been selling recycled homework for almost a decade. If they change the curriculum, you'll have to actually do the work again." There was a bite to Suzy's tone. She had never come to complete moral acceptance of Billy's selling homework to high school and college kids. Sure, Billy's family was poor as dirt so he had to do something to earn money, and he never sold answers to tests, but it still didn't feel right to her. Or maybe she hated the bullies he sold to so much that she wished Billy wouldn't help them so they'd fail quicker.

"We'll see," said Billy without a trace of concern in his voice.

THE REST OF THE SUMMER passed without anything to write home about. Suzy spent her usual week away for a family reunion at Pawley's Island, South Carolina. Billy always hated that week of summer. On one of those days, he ran into General Quinofski outside of a pizza place when he should have been away with his family.

"Hi, General, sir," he said. "Are you all back from vacation?"

Suzy's dad was so startled, he nearly dropped the pizza he was trying to balance while opening his car door. "Oh, hi Billy. Sorry, it's just me."

"Oh." Billy's head dropped with his voice. He flipped a pedal on his bicycle with his foot.

"I miss her, too, but the world's gone crazy, and it's my job to try to put some things right."

"Good luck with that, sir."

"Thanks, Billy."

Billy pedaled away, thinking of all the news stories he'd heard about international terrorists and internal investigations by the Senate on military loyalty. Try though he might, he couldn't understand any of it. That always puzzled him. How could a kid as smart as he was not understand the nightly news? The General said the world had gone crazy, but why? And why couldn't Billy shake the feeling that he had something to do with it?

The first day of school started with an assembly. Billy and Suzy were excited about the year. They were still the youngest kids on campus, having skipped two grades, but at least they knew their way around and where to sit in the auditorium. The new freshman class was relegated to the back of the balcony. Sophomores were in the balcony, too, but they got the front section. The juniors and seniors sat downstairs. Any speaker at an assembly worth his or her salt made sure to mention each class. Principal Dillon was no exception.

"I'd like to welcome our new freshman class." He paused for the polite applause of from the top of the balcony. "And our returning sophomores."

An explosion of cheers from the sophomores, including Billy and Suzy, taught the freshman how they were supposed to react. During this eruption, Billy and Suzy couldn't help but jump up and down together with excitement. They were not only cheering for their class, but for the start of their favorite thing in the world: school.

When the roar died down, Dillon cranked it up again. "Of course, you juniors…" He stopped while the students in the lower section of the auditorium took their turn to shake the building, which had gone through this structural test every year since its creation in 1923. When the juniors settled, Dillon said, "It will be your job to hold things together, because once they get their college acceptances, the senior class…" Dillon shouted over the loudest cheers yet, "WILL BE OUT OF CONTROL!"

He didn't have to wait for the college announcements. The seniors were already out of control. They knew it was their job to scream louder and longer than the other classes combined, even though their numbers were the smallest. This year's seniors had no trouble upholding their end of the school's long tradition.

Except, it wasn't tradition to start the year with an assembly.

"I've called this gathering because there have been some changes over the summer."

"Here we go," whispered Suzy. Her mom had done nothing but argue with people on the phone about school stuff all summer. Suzy read the local and national news like a hawk to keep up with what was happening, which she'd try to explain to Billy without much luck.

Dillon continued. "For one thing, you'll notice there are now security cameras in each of your classrooms, the halls, and the library. These cameras are for your safety. We hope they will put an end to bullying."

"Yeah, right," said Billy under his breath. When it came to bullies, Billy was an expert, having been their target all his life. He knew they would quickly find gaps in the camera coverage — like anywhere off the school grounds, or in social media. The cameras wouldn't stop bullying any more than turning on a light stops roaches. They just run to where you can't see them.

"Before too long," said Dillon, "you won't even know they are there."

Suzy looked around at the inattentiveness of her classmates. "More like they already don't care," she said.

"And we have new textbooks," said Dillon, "but I will let your teachers introduce those during each class."

"I told you so," said Suzy under her breath. "There goes your homework profit margin."

"C'mon, how much can math and physics change?"

"Yeah, that's true," said Suzy. "Shouldn't bother me too much, either. I mean, Biology is probably safe, right?"

"INTELLIGENT DESIGN!?"

Suzy was livid when she saw the chapter heading in her new biology textbook. She was on her feet protesting before the books were all handed out. "You're friggin' kidding me!"

"Suzy!" said Mr. Connors. From the level of his shock, Suzy realized she must not have said, "Friggin'."

"I'm sorry, Mr. Connors, but … really!?"

Mr. Connors' tone was sympathetic, but he had his job to do. "Suzy, I appreciate your passion, but we'll discuss that issue when—"

"No, we won't! *Katzmiller v. Dover* in 2005 says we don't have to discuss it. Not in public school."

"Snotski, what are you talking about?"

Suzy hadn't heard that nickname since middle school. She turned on platinum blonde (fake!) Lora Lantree — head cheerleader, most popular girl in school — and fired a retort out of reflex. "Look it up!"

"Yeah, I'll rush right out to the library and do that."

Mr. Connors chimed in before his first day of school got out of hand. "Settle! Both of you!" Suzy sat in anger. Lora got back to doodling a fingernail design in her notebook. "*Katzmiller v. Dover* … Lora!" He emphasized her name to get her attention. "Was a landmark court decision in 2005 that said intelligent design is not science, but religion, and therefore could not be included in a scientific text."

"Right," said Suzy, "so what's it doing in our new books? I mean, why not a chapter on the Wiccan Divine Great Goddess, or whatever." She apologized to the four Witches of Winston High, who sat silently in the back of class. "No offense."

"None taken," said Linda Lubinski, the head of the Coven. "Good idea."

"Science," said Mr. Connors, "does not exist in a vacuum." He glanced over his shoulder toward the ceiling.

Suzy saw one of the security cameras Dillon had mentioned, but didn't give it much thought. "This isn't—"

He stopped Suzy's protest with a raise of his hand. "There's an ebb and flow to knowledge, Suzy. It's like freedom. Knowledge is something that must be constantly fought for. And constantly defended."

"Then why aren't you defending it?"

A pained look filled Mr. Connors's face. He glanced up at the security camera again, then back to Suzy. "We have to choose our battles, Suzy."

Before she could respond, the bell rang, the class being shortened for the assembly schedule.

As she got up to leave, Suzy wasn't happy. She heard the words, but wasn't ready to accept the meaning. For the other kids, nothing had changed. They never knew what Mr. Connors was talking about with the old textbook, and they still didn't with the new one.

"KIDS!"

General Quinofski snapped, which was out of character for him. He had been patient while they filled him in on the new textbooks, but when they started talking about plans of action, he cut them off. "I'd love to help, but I'm up to my ears in a new Senate investigation."

"But—" started Suzy.

"Take it up with your mother. She has more pull in the schools anyway."

Billy wasn't a hundred percent sure what a Senate investigation was, but it couldn't be good. "Are you okay, General?"

Suzy's dad got his quick, confidence-inducing smile back. "I'm fine, son, just busy." He gave a deep sigh. "These things happen from time to time. It'll pass as soon as midterm elections are over."

Billy didn't keep up with politics, so he wasn't sure what Suzy's dad was talking about. He did know that, behind his smile, the General looked tired. Suzy gave Billy a "let's get out of here" head toss, and they went down to her lab.

"I warned you this would happen," said Suzy. "It was going on all summer. Mom's been talking about it. Tighter restrictions on curricula, teaching to standardized tests. I think every teacher in town has come by to beg her to come back to the School Board."

Billy was only half listening. "Why doesn't she?" he asked, but his mind was elsewhere.

"Term limits."

Absently, he said, "Oh."

"There's got to be something we can do," said Suzy. "I'm not going to have my year wasted by ignorant book publishers with a big Washington lobby."

"You sound like your parents."

"What's wrong with that?"

She expected Billy to be right there with her, supporting the cause of a proper education, but instead he was standing in the doorway staring out at nothing.

"Billy...?"

"Something's wrong. I don't know what it is, but something is very wrong."

TWO

DREAM A LITTLE DREAM

"**H**I, I'M EVIL."

Billy knew he was dreaming in that dual reality way that can only be felt in a dream. Part of him knew it was a dream, and wasn't scared. Part of him didn't, and was.

The person talking to him reminded Billy of some kind of slick cartoon character, but he couldn't figure out which one. He was very old, but dressed young in a sharp purple suit, an oversized hat, and an attitude that exuded confidence and evaporated trust. While Billy stood in a field of rich grass and flowers, the man leaned against a dirty brick wall at the end of a dark alley.

"I'm sorry, you're who?" asked Billy.

The cartoon man spoke with an accent that sounded like the guys in *The Sopranos*, which Billy had learned about from his brother, Peter. "I said, 'I'm Evil, and I was wondering if you'd like to join me'."

"Don't be stupid! You just told me you're evil, why would I want to join you?"

Billy noticed the guy had been flipping a coin, because right then he stopped doing it. "Good point." The man put the coin in his pocket and a one-foot-long toothpick in his mouth. The wooden stick looked familiar to Billy, but he wasn't sure why. "You're a smart kid. I'm going to have to change my recruiting tactics, huh?"

"Don't do anything on my account."

The man pushed off the wall and started walking into the darkness of the alley, talking to himself along the way. "Don't tell people I'm Evil. Good idea. What should I tell 'em, I wonder?" Over his shoulder, he shot a smile that sent such a chill down Billy's spine. It snapped him awake.

The Evil Grin.

"You need to wake up, Billy."

Billy jumped so far out of his bed that, if he were a cat, he'd be hanging upside down on the ceiling by his claws. Since he wasn't a cat, he stuffed himself into the corner of the room, pulling the covers up to his eyeballs.

The old man who told him to wake up sat in his desk chair, wearing a gray robe and drumming his fingers on Billy's desk. "The problems of two 13-year-old kids may not amount to a hill of beans in this crazy world, but only you can solve them, Billy."

Billy felt a weight on his shoulders that he didn't think he could bear.

The old man began to fade away like a ghost. "Wake up!"

THE SOUND OF THE *Today Show* on his mother's 1970s color TV replaced the eerie feeling from the dream. Every morning Billy's mom played the ancient thing loud enough to wake the dead while she got ready for her Walmart job.

One of the substitute reporters on the show read the news. "The science community is mourning the loss of Dr. Will Parkson today…"

Billy bolted into the living room to hear the rest.

"…who died of an apparent suicide. Parkson won the Nobel Prize in Physics for his discovery of the 'orphan layer' of single paired particles, which marks the boundary of our universe and proves that matter existed before the Big Bang. He also hosted various science-related TV shows."

Billy sank into the couch. Parkson had been a hero of his. Someone he'd hoped to work with one day, not because he was a TV personality, but because of his brilliance in astrophysics. Billy felt the loss of great potential for the world of knowledge.

"WHY DO YOU THINK you dreamed about joining Evil?"

Billy thought Dr. Weston missed the point, but he wasn't exactly sure what it was either. "I didn't. I mean, I don't want to become evil. I believe in science and truth; making the world a better place, and all of that stuff."

Unless, of course, Evil could get him out of going to these stupid sessions at the police station.

Billy thought that; he didn't say it. He didn't mean it. He just hated having to give up his open first period class to meet with a psychiatrist — no matter how much Suzy told him it was cool. She loved anything to do with the brain. Billy was fine with that, as long as it wasn't his brain she was talking about.

"And what about this old man?" asked Weston.

"That didn't feel like a dream."

"But it was?"

"Yeah," said Billy. "I guess it had to be."

"He said that you're responsible for the problems of the world?"

Billy cocked his head. Her question didn't sound right. "No. He told me that only I could solve the problems of the world."

"Do you believe that?"

"No, of course not." This time his own words didn't sound right. "I mean, I believe that science can solve a lot of the world's problems, and I want to be a scientist, so in a way, yes."

"But you, personally, don't have to solve the world's problems, right? Just science in general."

"Yeah, of course." Billy picked at his bottom of his shirt. "What do you think the dreams mean?"

Dr. Weston sighed and took off her glasses. "Sometimes a dream is just a dream, but how we react to them can tell us something about ourselves."

"Do you think I reacted okay?"

The young doctor smiled. "I'm supposed to say, 'It doesn't matter what I think, but how you feel.'"

"I'm fine with it."

"Me, too."

"But what does the dream mean?"

"I don't know, Billy. Interpreting dreams is an inexact

science at best. I try to stay away from it."

"But it has to mean something." Billy never liked unanswered questions.

"If you want to try to dig into it yourself, remember what happens in a dream is almost always a metaphor for something else. It's an image of something your brain is trying to figure out."

"I don't know," said Billy. "Evil was pretty clear about being evil."

Dr. Weston changed the subject. "How is life with your mom these days?"

"Fine." Billy always hated this part of their sessions. Of all the subjects on his long list of things he didn't want to talk about, his mom was at the top.

"I looked a little further into your records and found her arrest for assaulting an officer, causing a disturbance, and—"

Billy cut her off. "Yeah, I know. I was there." Her breakdown was the worst day in Billy's life up to that point. He had no desire to relive it.

Dr. Weston took on a wise-beyond-her-20-something years tone. "Living with a schizophrenic can be exhausting, and scary, and ... horrible, and a whole lot of things that I can only imagine. I had to treat a few of them in college, and, well... you have my sympathies. Especially when it's someone you love. That can be very hard, Billy."

"She's been okay, lately. She's taking her meds, and she seems to think the evil yard gnomes have been banished by some kind of invisible force field I created."

"There's that word again."

"What?"

"Evil."

BILLY DIDN'T TALK to Suzy about his dream until their daily walk home from school. He didn't want to slip and mention his psychiatry appointment anywhere near another school kid.

The subject of dreams got her started on her own. "I had a crazy dream about a black cat."

Billy picked up a stick, twirled it in his hand, checked its balance, while half-listening to Suzy.

"The cat was really weird. For some reason, I got the feeling it was as smart as we are — maybe smarter — and that it was trying to tell me something."

Billy was going to say Evil seemed intelligent, too, but was interrupted by the familiar low growl of his brother's tricked-out 1967 Dodge Charger cruising by. A cackle of laughter cut through the sound of the pistons. Billy saw Linda Lubinski, the leader of the Witches of Winston High, riding shotgun. Though Billy would never admit it, there was something about her pale skin, raven-black hair, and a slew of other things that made him feel wiggly inside.

Something about her riding in his 20-year-old brother's car made him angry and hurt. He absently broke the stick he'd picked up.

Suzy couldn't help but notice Billy's deflated mood. "They're dating, you know."

"Yeah, I got that feeling when I was at her house."

Suzy raised an eyebrow. "What? When were you at her house?"

Billy thought about it, but couldn't come up with any details. "I don't know. A while back."

"What were you doing there?"

"I don't know. Peter sent me there for something."

They walked in silence for a few steps. Suzy mistook Billy's quiet demeanor as a reaction to his brother dating a girl he had a crush on. "I don't know why you're so upset. Linda's a senior. She's eighteen. You're thirteen. I don't think it would work out. Besides, she's never given you the time of day."

"It's not that."

"And, there are three others in the Coven just as funky as she is, if that's the kind of girl you like."

"Why do you care what kind of girl I like?"

Suzy snapped. "I don't! Believe me, I really don't."

"Fine. I believe you."

Suzy huffed, puffed, and stormed into her house and slammed the door.

"What!?" asked Billy to her closed front door. When she didn't answer, he went home without a clue.

BILLY FOUND HIS MOTHER clipping coupons from the paper, which would be fine, except she was folding and stacking the pages with squares and rectangles cut out of them.

"Mom! You are not going to start saving cut-up newspaper again!"

"But Billy-boy," she said as if her baby still was one. "I need the papers. They have important things in them."

"Mom, I did not clean up this entire trailer so you could fill it with junk again."

Billy's mom got her hackles up. "I can do whatever I like in my own home, especially after you and your brother threw out all of my treasures without so much as asking me! That was a hurtful thing to do to me, Billy. Hurtful."

Billy ignored her, staring into the corner of the room as if some enlightenment might have just ducked behind the couch. He was trying to remember exactly when and how he and Peter cleaned the house. Sure, they'd done it years ago, when Suzy and a bunch of Peter's friends pitched in, but his Mom had filled it to overflowing with garbage since then. He remembered his mother being very upset when she found it clean, but he had no idea how it got that way.

"Is Peter home?" he asked, but didn't wait for an answer. "Peter!?"

Peter shouted from his makeshift garage outside. "What?"

Billy went to the blue-tarp-covered addition to the trailer that functioned as Peter's oasis away from his mother and nerdy brother. He was, as usual, under his car doing Lord knows what, since everything about it had been pitch-perfect for years.

Billy spoke to a pair of feet sticking out from under the chrome trim. "Do you remember cleaning up the house last year?"

"Nope, 'cause I didn't. You did."

"But how did I do it? When did I do it? You know we can't so much as throw away a napkin while Mom's home, and she never leaves the house."

"I don't know, brat. I came home and the place was clean."

"YOU DON'T REMEMBER cleaning the house?"

Billy had decided that, if he had to see a psychiatrist, he might as well make the most of it. He told her about his hording mother and how their mobile home somehow got cleaned up, but he didn't remember how. "No, I don't remember," he said to Dr. Weston, "I remember the house being a mess, and I remember Mom becoming a screaming lunatic when she found out it was cleaned up, but I don't remember anything in between."

Dr. Weston furrowed her brow, which Billy was learning meant she wasn't sure what to say next. "It's possible … or, you tell me, is it possible that you cleaned it in your sleep? People do amazing things while sleepwalking."

Billy shook his head. "No way. It took about ten of us three days to clean it up a few years ago, and the mess wasn't half as bad as it was recently."

Dr. Weston was stumped. She flipped through Billy's file looking for some explanation. "Did I see here…?" She found it. "Yes, your mother was hospitalized around this time, wasn't she?"

"Yeah," said Billy. "Why couldn't I forget that?" Memories of the worst night of his life made him twist in his chair: Her screams about the evil yard gnomes trying to take "her baby," a.k.a. him. The police tasing him and pepper-spraying everyone. Linda Lubinski witnessing his humiliation. Then there was the strange behavior of the patients in the mental ward, all of them telling him and Suzy to "break the connection."

Dr. Weston snapped him out of his day-mare. "That must have been very traumatic."

"Yeah."

"Memory is a funny thing, Billy. It's possible that, in your grief, while your mother was away, you manically scrubbed the house clean, and your memory as well."

"I suppose that's possible," Billy said, but he didn't believe it.

BILLY SAT ALONE in his room. This wasn't unusual. It was how he spent most of his time. His brother was out with friends. He could hear his mother on the porch drinking and talking to herself. Life was as it always had been.

Then it wasn't. A clap of thunder rocked Billy's mobile home and knocked him to the floor. Before he could even guess what was happening, he heard a familiar voice.

"Hello, Billy."

He looked up to see Dr. Menaus standing in front of his closet, holding a five-foot-long wooden staff.

His mother called from the porch. "Billy! Did they get you? Are you there?"

Before Billy could answer, Dr. Menaus raised his staff and said, "Sleep." A bright white light flashed out from the stick in all directions. Billy heard a thud from the porch. Menaus must have seen the concern on Billy's face. "It's all right, son. She's just sleeping."

"What's happening?"

"Give it a second, your memories will come back."

Sure enough, Billy's head filled with images he didn't fully understand — but as they came and went, understanding followed. He and Suzy working together on a magic wand. Peter even helped. Billy disappeared. The terror of his first trip into the Quantum World weakened his knees. If he weren't already on the floor, he would have fallen over. Instead, he felt the carpet, his bed, his desk, his chair. They were real and solid. He must still be in his room, but…

"How did you get here?" he asked Dr. Menaus.

"Glad to see my memory spells are holding up." He answered Billy's question with dramatic flair. "Dr. Menaus made a magic wand."

"You stole my idea."

"Yes, well, that's your word against mine, Billy, and after our little conversation you're not going to remember that I was here or that you made a magic wand, so it's kind of a moot point, isn't it?"

With lost memories still finding homes in his head, Billy wasn't in good enough shape to argue with Menaus. He was lucky that he had the strength to drag himself to his feet.

Dr. Menaus casually sat on the edge of Billy's little school desk. Clearly, he didn't care about Billy's situation. He had his own agenda. "I had a discussion with a friend of yours, Billy, an old man with long grey hair and a beard to match."

Billy flashed on his conversations with this quantum being. "The Teacher," he said to himself.

"Is that what you call him? I call him the old idiot." Menaus leaned on his staff. "He had all kinds of warnings about the power of the magic, and dark forces, blah, blah."

Billy's own recollections of the Teacher hadn't fully formed, but he didn't think he was an idiot. He didn't say as much to Menaus, mostly because his scrambled head made it difficult for him to say much at all.

"I had another visitor that I like a lot better. He didn't tell me his name—"

"Quantum Beings don't have names," said Billy right before he remembered his conversation with his familiar in a seedy hotel room. "Not like we have them."

"Yeah, that's kind of a bother, isn't it? Anyway, this other guy said I could keep my wand as long as I like, and that I could do anything I want with it, so long as I did him just one favor."

Menaus casually ran a finger over Billy's small desk, as if checking it for dust. Obviously, he wasn't going to continue the conversation until Billy asked, "What favor?" which he did.

"I just have to keep you from getting your wand back."

Until a minute ago, Billy didn't know he had a magic wand, so he had to fast-forward through confusing scenes from a life he didn't know he'd lived to get to the part where he had thrown his wand away in disgust, wishing he'd never made the thing. He didn't know where it was now, but assumed it was somewhere in the Quantum World, exactly where it's not supposed to be. He finally asked, "How do you plan to do that?"

"Well, my new imaginary friend says I should kill you."

Billy started to laugh off the idea of Dr. Menaus committing murder, when suddenly Menaus's face flashed before him. Fear welled up in Billy's chest. He tried to remember the fight he'd had with Menaus, the one that got Billy arrested. The one he'd been told he had, but had no memory of. Try as he might, he still couldn't find that memory. Meanwhile, his vision of Menaus continued. The professor screamed, his staff held over his head, and swung it down at Billy.

Billy ducked.

Menaus laughed. When Billy looked up, he saw that Menaus hadn't moved. He was still sitting on his desk as casually as ever, and said, "Don't worry, I think murder is a bit extreme, don't you?"

Billy didn't know if the strange vision of Menaus attacking him was a memory or hallucination, but it didn't matter. It instilled in him a deep understanding that Menaus was capable of some serious violence.

"But that's not really what I came to talk to you about. I mean, as long as I can wipe your memory, you're not going to bother looking for your wand. You can't find what you didn't know existed in the first place, right?" Menaus got up and paced the room. "The reason I wanted to talk to you was because," he held out his staff, "I don't really know how this thing works."

When Billy didn't say anything, he went back to leaning on his oversized walking stick. "I saw how you told Suzy to 'think about her lab' before you disappeared, and she had said that you learned 'thoughts are real.' I took from that, the wand taps into the electrical impulses of your thoughts and," he waved his hands like a cartoon magician, "hee-bee gee-bee, somehow your thoughts become reality. But it doesn't always work, right?"

Billy didn't think about whether he has helping an enemy or a mad man. He was still busy putting two and two together in his head. "It has its own logic," he said.

"I'm starting to figure that out," said Menaus. "Like, the other day; I was remembering my friends from grad school. How we sat around talking about what kind of fancy cars we would get when we were rich and famous scientists — like that would ever happen."

The way he said that last bit, Billy got the feeling he was supposed to laugh, but he didn't. There was too much bitterness in Menaus's voice to make it a joke.

Menaus went on. "Except, it did kind of happen with one of us. Dr. Will Parkson."

Billy knew that name. "He discovered the edge of the universe by finding an outer band of orphaned paired particles."

"Yeah, him."

"He has his own TV show, right?" There was some other important thing about Parkson that Billy couldn't remember.

"Not anymore," said Menaus. "He's dead."

"What!?" That was the other thing.

"He'd always wanted a 1963 Corvette Sting Ray. I'd tell him, 'it's a common car. What you should get is a '66 Shelby Cobra.' So, anyway, I was thinking about that conversation and the '63 Corvette, so I figured why don't I just whip myself up one with my wand, right?"

"Why not the Cobra?" asked Billy,

Menaus answered by pointing his finger at Billy and giving him an accusing look. That's when Billy caught the smell of whiskey on his breath. He knew it well from his mother.

"That's…" Menaus trailed off. "That's not an answer

I want to consider right now. Let me finish my story."

For a kid his age, Billy had way too much experience with adults who had had too much to drink — though, this was the first time one of them was armed with a miracle weapon. Still, it didn't change his well-worn tactic of shutting up and letting them talk.

"So I think about Will and his stupid Corvette, and I fire the wand. BAM! Suddenly, a mint condition car is sitting in my backyard with Will inside, behind the wheel, dead as a doornail. 'Mind! I don't mean to say that I know, of my own knowledge, what there is particularly dead about a doornail.'"

Menaus paused as if he expected Billy to say something, but Billy stuck to his strategy of silence.

"Sorry, that's Dickens." He gestured with his walking stick. "You know what the funny part is? I'm not upset about it. I hated Will Parkson. Now he's dead, and I might be the one who killed him. I don't know. I don't care. You know what I did?"

Again, no response from Billy.

"No? Okay, I'll tell you. I zapped him and his car into his living room and left the motor running. Then I did a little research and changed his blood chemistry to make his cause of death carbon monoxide poisoning. You might have heard about it on the news. Funny, I was tempted not to do the bit with the blood chemistry. I'd love to know what his real cause of death was."

Billy could hold his tongue no longer. Parkson was one of the world's great thinkers. There no telling what his knowledge might have done to help mankind. Menaus had killed him on a whim without a shred of regret. "You thought him to death."

"No, I didn't. Billy, the wand killed him. Why did it do that?"

"You can tell yourself that, but you wished for the Corvette because you wanted to hurt him. The wand knows your real thoughts and feelings. That's what it makes come true."

Menaus let out a casual, "Humph," looked at his magic walking stick, then perked up. "Oh, well, lesson learned. Thanks for the talk, Billy, but now it's time that you…" He pointed his staff toward Billy and pressed the button, "…forget."

"BILLY, I'M GLAD you're here," said Suzy.

Billy wasn't quite sure where "here" was, which was followed shortly by the realization that he was in another dream. He tried to recall when exactly it was he'd gone to sleep. Was he still in class? No. He had had an uneventful day. He came home, went to his room, read *Scientific American* online, posted some comments, prepared all the homework he'd promised to sell the next day, and… yeah, he went to bed at his normal time and was now sitting in an apple tree outside of Suzy's house. She was in the tree with him and had just told him she was glad he was here.

"This is the cat I was telling you about." Sure enough, next to Suzy was an uppity black cat. "Watch," said Suzy. "She'll turn into a girl."

As soon as she said that, the cat transformed into a tomboy of a girl wearing a cartoonish black and white horizontally striped top, a red neckerchief, and a black beret. The cat-turned-girl flipped them a snooty expression and said, "Le meow."

Billy spooked like a horse, slipped, and fell out of the tree. The falling sensation woke him up.

THIS SCHOOL YEAR, the same as last, Billy, Suzy, and the Witches of Winston High had study hall together in Mrs. Nelson's class. It was widely reported that Mrs. Nelson would turn down her hearing aids at the beginning of study hall so she could read her magazines in peace. There had to be some truth to this rumor, since she had a reputation of being as mean as a snake during her regular classes, but in study hall, so long as the kids didn't start a riot or a fire, they could do pretty much whatever they liked.

The day after the cat dream, Suzy waited for Mrs. Nelson to settle down with her magazines and touch the inside of her ear, where she wore her hearing aid. Suzy then jumped around in her chair to interrupt Billy's ogling of the Coven. "Billy, you were in my dream last night."

"That's funny," said Billy, "because I had a dream about you, too."

"Isn't that sweet," said Linda.

"They dream about each other," said Mary.

"They are an adorable couple," said Lisa.

"Absolutely," said Sonni.

Suzy snapped out with a little too much enthusiasm. "We are not a couple!"

"Oh, right," said Linda.

"Sorry," said Mary.

"We know you're just friends," said Sonni.

"Yeah, 'just friends,'" said Lisa, like she didn't mean it.

Suzy pointedly turned her back on the Coven. "Anyway, Billy, you were in my dream."

"With the cat?" asked Billy.

"Yes, with the cat. And we were—"

"In an apple tree?"

"Oh my God, yes!"

The two people in school least likely to ever have the Witches of Winston High's attention had it full on.

"The Tree of Knowledge," said Sonni.

"Was there a snake?" asked Mary.

Linda shushed them, and together the Coven sat on the edges of their seats.

"No snake, just the cat," said Billy.

"And the cat," said Suzy, "turned into—"

"A French girl." Billy and Suzy said together.

Suzy continued. "And she said..."

Together, "Le Meow."

Three

A Test of Magic

U NCHARACTERISTICALLY, LISA CHANG spoke out of turn. "Whoa, that was some powerful magic."

"They're faking it," said Linda.

Billy and Suzy stared at each other in silent contemplation. Should they laugh it off? Pretend they were joking? "I wish we were," said Billy. Lying wasn't their style.

"You're telling me that you two shared the same dream?" Linda asked.

Again, Billy and Suzy weren't sure what to say. After another long silent stare, Suzy said, "It looks that way."

"Wow," said Mary.

"I've heard of that," said Sonni.

"But it's rare," said Lisa.

"Yeah, like, almost never," said Linda. Her tone was

more of surprise than skepticism. "That is some pow-erful magic."

"It's not magic," said Billy. He and the Coven had been over this subject a thousand times.

"Then what is it?" ask Linda.

"I don't know," said Billy, "but calling it 'magic' means you're giving up on finding out what really happened."

"What do you think?"

It took Suzy a second to realize Linda was talking to her. In all the time they'd known each other, Linda had barely ever acknowledged her existence. Suzy finally responded, "Billy is comparing magic to miracles."

"Miracles are cruel," said Billy.

Suzy jumped in to clarify. "He means that… say someone survives a disease that has a one hundred percent mortality rate. If you call that a miracle, then you're giving up on the ninety-nine other victims."

Mary got lost somewhere between disease and mortality rate. "What?"

"In science we'd call that an anomaly," Suzy explained, "and try to find out exactly why it happened, so we could cure everyone else."

"Why couldn't the anomaly be caused by magic?" asked Sonni, who kept an easy pace with Suzy's argument.

"Because there is no such thing as magic," said Billy.

Linda pointed at him. "Here you have, right in front of you, proof-positive of magic, and you won't admit it."

"No," said Billy. "Here we have an event that we haven't investigated. It could be as simple as Suzy already told me about her dream and we both forgot about it."

Suzy mumbled almost to herself. "It's the first time we've talked today."

Linda pressed her side of the argument. "What is it going to take to make you believe in magic?"

"I don't know," said Billy. "How about if you cast a spell that does something completely impossible."

"Like what?" asked Mary.

"I don't know," said Billy. "Make me flunk my calculus test next period." He knew he'd ace that test, and because it was coming up in a few minutes, they wouldn't be able to pull any tricks.

"Fine," said Linda.

Together, all four Witches of Winston High looked to Mrs. Nelson. Her nose was buried in some cooking magazine, oblivious to life. The girls got up and snuck out of the back door.

"Okay, it's not magic," said Suzy when they were gone. "But it's weird, yeah?"

"Totally weird."

"BILLY BOBBLE!"

He couldn't help but stare. It was the strangest thing, to see a black cat sitting on Craig Westbrook's desk in the middle of a test. Billy was so befuddled by the cat, he didn't notice Mr. Hobbs standing in front of him calling his name.

"Billy Bobble, you're cheating!"

That got his attention. "What?!" He took his eye off the cat and instantly knew it wouldn't be there when he turned back.

"You were looking at Mr. Westbrook's test."

"Don't be stupid, Mr. Hobbs—"

"—What did you call me?"

Not the right thing to say. "I mean, I gave Craig the answers to this test weeks ago." Also, not the right thing to say.

Mr. Hobbs pointed to them both. "You two. Principal Dillon's office. Now!"

"BILLY, I'M DISAPPOINTED in you."

Mr. Dillon meant what he said. Billy and Suzy were the shining stars of his career. He'd known Billy for over five years, ever since he started helping the football team with their homework. They had a "don't ask, don't tell" policy on the details of how Billy helped them. As far as Dillon was concerned, Billy was their tutor. Any rumors that he was selling homework were just that – malicious lies told by people wanting to find a way to keep Winston High's star athletes out of the game. Thanks to Billy, Winston High was a perennial sports and academic powerhouse. Plus, Billy created the school's database software. Dillon lived in fear of the day Billy would no longer be around to maintain it.

"I wasn't cheating, Mr. Dillon, honest."

Dillon was ready to sweep this whole thing under the rug. "If Billy says he wasn't cheating, that's good enough for me."

"Mr. Dillon," said Mr. Hobbs, which made Billy wonder if teachers called each other Mister and Mizz all the time, or only when kids were around. "I observed Mr. Bobble staring at Mr. Westbrook's test paper, and when I confronted Mr. Bobble, he said I was stupid."

"I didn't say that," said Billy. He pled his case to Mr. Dillon. "I said, 'don't be stupid.'"

"Which implies," said Hobbs, "that I was being stupid. Don't tell me when I have and have not been insulted, Mr. Bobble."

Dillon took off his reading glasses and rubbed his eyes. Billy wasn't sure, but he thought Dillon might be hiding a smile. "Actually, Hobbs, thinking that Billy would need to get a calculus answer off of Craig's test isn't the brightest thing I've heard you say." Dillon then said to Craig. "No offense, Craig."

"None taken, sir."

Dillon continued his apology. "Just being in calculus by your senior year says you're a smart kid, but…"

"Yeah, but I'm no Billy Bobble." On the playground, said by a jock, that would have been an insult, but Craig's tone was all respect. Billy blushed a bit.

Dillon continued with Mr. Hobbs. "So, I doubt that—"

"That's not why we're here." Hobbs interrupted. "I can and will fail Bobble for not keeping his eyes on his paper, whether he cheated or not…"

For the first time, Billy felt fear well up inside of him. Not that he might get in trouble, but that somehow this had to do with the spell cast by the Coven. He felt out of control, and that didn't sit right. If the Coven could actually change events with only thoughts and words, then nothing in life made sense.

Hobbs was still talking. "Bobble said that he had given Mr. Westbrook the answers to the test weeks ago."

Dillon put his hands together like a church steeple and pressed his index fingers to his lips in thought.

Hobbs checked left and right, as if someone might be listening, then leaned forward. "Jack, you know how closely they're watching us."

Dillon said nothing.

"This could mean both of our jobs."

Dillon's forehead wrinkled. He folded his arms over his chest and sighed. He took another breath before he said, "Billy, when you said you'd given Craig the answers to the test, what did you mean?"

There was an inflection in Dillon's voice that Billy didn't understand. It was like everyone in the room knew the answer to the question and the answer Billy was supposed to give, and that they weren't necessarily the same thing. Everyone, but Billy that is. "Uh…"

"You've been tutoring, Craig." Dillon's question was more of a statement, and Billy saw the opportunity being handed to him.

"Yes, of course." Billy suddenly realized why this was such a big issue. "I never flat out sell the answers to tests. That would be cheating."

"And you're not a cheater," said Dillon. "You're a tutor. You tutor lots of students, don't you, Billy?"

"Yes, sir."

Dillon spread his hands out to Hobbs. "Nothing wrong with that, is there Mr. Hobbs?"

"I suppose not," he said. "But I still have to fail Billy for not keeping his eyes on his paper."

"That's your prerogative," said Dillon. "It's also your prerogative to give a makeup test, is it not?"

"It is."

Dillon asked Billy, "Would that suit you?"

"Absolutely. I like tests." As he said that, Billy realized the Coven had passed theirs. Their magic had worked.

"I SAW THE CAT."

Billy didn't bother telling Misters Hobbs or Dillon about the cat. He knew no one would believe him, and a kid that has to do mandatory psychiatry sessions once a week really shouldn't spout off about invisible cats. But he could tell Suzy on their walk home from school. She would understand. That's what their walks were for.

"Was it the same cat from our dream?" she asked.

"I think so. I mean, a black cat is pretty much a black cat, you know?"

They walked in silence for a full minute before Suzy broached the subject. "Do you think...?"

"No! I do not think their spell had anything to do with it."

"Well, what then?"

"I don't know." But Billy did know what Suzy was thinking. His mother's a paranoid schizophrenic. It could run in the family. He started a new line of thought. "If it wasn't for our shared dream, I'd say..."

Suzy didn't let him finish. "You're right. It's not you."

The great relief in her voice confirmed Billy's suspicion that she thought it might have been him.

"Something is going on," she said with way too much enthusiasm for Billy's taste.

"So what do we do about it?"

Suzy was a bit surprised she was the one to have to

tell Billy. "We approach it like scientists. We try to repeat the anomaly."

"You mean…?""

"I'll see you in your dreams."

Before Billy could respond, they heard voices coming from Suzy's house.

"There are rules, Jack!"

"To hell with the rules!"

Much to Billy and Suzy's surprise, they knew who the bellows belonged to. The first wasn't a shocker except for the intensity. Billy didn't recall ever hearing Suzy's mom raise her voice. The other was the one they didn't expect.

Suzy put her finger to her lips and dragged Billy under an open living room window. "I didn't know Principal Dillon's first name was Jack," she whispered.

Billy nodded and whispered back. "His wife would call him that after hours when I was working on the school database."

Suzy put her finger to her lips again.

Mrs. Q. said, "You're preaching to the choir, Jack, but they have a majority on the board and made it clear that they want term limits. That means I'm out."

"I don't understand the logic of forcing someone out of a job because they have done it well enough to keep it for a long time," said Dillon. "They're always talking about running government like a corporation. Well, what company fires successful CEOs for having experience?"

"It's an off-shoot of 'Absolute power corrupts absolutely.'" That voice belonged to Suzy's Dad. "But Lord Acton was talking about popes and kings, not elected officials."

"My point, exactly," said Dillon.

"I'm sorry, Jack, I really am," said Mrs. Quinofski. "Is it as bad as that?"

The kids heard a heavy sigh, then Dillon said, "If it was just the local school board, I could handle it. If it was just some federal politicians trying to drum up votes, I could handle that, too. But they have gotten together like they never have before. They are moving at lightning speed. It's like they are thinking with one brain."

Mrs. Quinofski said, "Why is it that the ones who know the least about education are always the ones trying to fix it?"

"If it's any consolation," said General Quinofski, "we're having the same problem in the military. Small minds in big places, all working with lockstep efficiency."

"Opinions based on ignorance have become the basis of policy," said Mrs. Quinofski, "instead of theories supported by facts."

"I taught her that one," whispered Suzy.

Billy whispered back, "I guess we're not the only ones who think there's something wrong in the world."

BILLY FOUND HIMSELF standing in the middle of his bedroom. It was nearly midnight. He couldn't remember how he got there. He recalled walking home from Suzy's house, watching TV, and ... nothing else. What's more, there was a familiar smell of men's cologne. Though the smell was familiar, it seemed out of place in his family's mobile home.

Something else bothered Billy. He had to do something important. What was it?

Oh, yes! His experiment with Suzy. He crawled into bed and soon fell asleep.

In his dream, Billy floated in space, looking down on a planet beneath him. It was earth. From where he was, Billy could block out the whole world with his thumb. He also realized that he wasn't inside a spaceship, or a suit for that matter, which made him wonder out loud. "How can I hear myself talk in space?"

"Cool, isn't it?"

Suzy's voice came from right beside him, but she wasn't in space. She was standing on a circular observation deck looking over the railing. Billy then realized he was, too. Neither one of them were in space, but rather in a hospital over an operating room — like something from an old horror movie.

Beneath them, Billy's mother lay as a patient. "Hi, baby!" She waved at the kids.

"Mom? Are you okay?"

"Oh, I'm fine," she said, and she sounded it for the first time in as long as Billy could remember. Her voice did not quiver in fear of being overheard by evil spirits. She did not sound robotic, like when she was on meds. She sounded perfectly normal, which for Billy wasn't normal at all. "In fact," she went on, "I'm the only one around here who is fine."

"Then why are you having an operation?"

"They want to cut out my memory, so I can be like everyone else."

"Mom! No!"

"It's okay, Billy. Being the only one to remember things is exhausting. Everyone thinks I'm crazy."

The surgeon — or at least Billy thought he must be the surgeon because he wore scrubs and seemed more authoritative than the other person in the room — looked up at Billy. The man was impossibly old. Long gray hair stretched out from under his green surgical cap, as did a gray beard from the mask that dangled around his chin. "Nurse?" He made a downward gesture with his hand that Billy took to mean, put her under.

"Nighty, night, Billy," said his mother.

The one called nurse turned a knob on the hospital bed and his mom drifted into sleep.

Suzy nudged him. "Billy! The nurse. That's the French cat-girl!"

Sure enough, it was the same girl who had morphed herself from a cat to a French girl. She winked at both of them and made a playful clawing motion with her hand.

"Suzy!" The surgeon's voice was deep and commanding. "Our patient has cancer. How do we cure cancer?"

Suzy didn't miss a beat. She was in her element here. Sure, she preferred microbiology, but it all tied together. "You have to kill the cancer cells."

"Fine," said the teaching surgeon. "Nurse, kill the patient."

"No!" shouted Billy and Suzy at the same time.

"Why not?" asked the surgeon. "If we kill the patient, the cancer will die as well."

Suzy answered. "You have to find a way to get rid of the bad cells, without hurting the good ones."

"Ah, *Primum non nocere*," said the surgeon.

"Yes," Suzy translated. "'First do no harm.'"

"Fine. Nurse, cancel the operation."

"Wait," said Billy. "If she's got cancer, she may need the operation."

The old surgeon thought about this for a moment, then turned to the other side of the observation room. "General?"

Billy and Suzy followed his gaze to see Suzy's dad teaching a class full of cadets and old men and women in suits. "There are enemies in the world," said General Quinofski.

The older people stamped their walking canes on the floor and shouted, "Here! Here!" Billy and Suzy wondered where the canes came from. Then they wondered how they both knew what they were wondering.

"There are people who want to do evil things," the General continued, "and we must stop them."

"Absolutely!" shouted the cane-carrying men and women.

"But how we do that is important," said the General. His students hushed. "How much harm we do to ourselves in the name of curing the cancer that lives among us determines how successful the cancer is."

His students were befuddled. Not knowing where to turn, they looked over the railing to the surgeon and his patient.

Billy and Suzy did the same and saw that his mother's head had been replaced with the planet earth. It was as big as his mom's head used to be, which was also as big as it was when he was floating in space.

"Oh, look!" said the nurse. "She's turning red."

Sure enough, Billy and Suzy could see the North American continent that was his mother's face, turning

R.S. Mellette

bright red. The surgeon inspected his patient, then said to the kids, "Very scary."

"What does that mean?" asked Billy.

The nurse ignored his question and said to the doctor, "Makes me miss *E Pluribus Unum*."

The surgeon answered Billy's question. "Ask your history teacher."

The kids were so eager for an answer that they leaned hard over the railing of the observation room. At that moment, it gave way, and they went tumbling toward the sterile tile floor.

BILLY WOKE UP on what would have been impact if the dream had been real. Wet with sweat, it took him a moment to realize that his phone was buzzing.

It was a text message from Suzy: "Write it down before you forget. Don't talk about it with anyone, and we'll compare notes in study hall."

Billy's thoughts came out in a single, quiet, word. "Wow."

Four

THE WITCH HUNT

"NO WAY!"

Linda snatched Billy's dream notes from his hand before he and Suzy had a chance to compare them.

Mary put her hand out to Suzy, who looked at Billy.

"Might as well," he said. "At least it's a third-party opinion."

Linda started reading Billy's notes. "'I floated in geosynchronous orbit at one of the five Lagrangian points between the earth and moon.'" She stopped reading. "Jesus, Billy, even your dreams read like a textbook. You've got to learn to have a little fun."

"I have fun," started Billy, but he was shushed by the rest of the Coven.

Mary read from Suzy's notes. "'It started as a flying dream.'" She looked up. "I love those."

"That's a sign of strong magic," said Sonni. Suzy ignored the invitation to argue the point.

Mary got back to reading. "I flew down the spine of a giant DNA double-helix."

"They both dream in textbook," said Lisa.

"They really are born for each other," said Sonni.

Once again, Mary took up the reading. "The DNA turned out to be a giant piece of art outside some kind of teaching hospital, where I suddenly found myself in the balcony of a surgical—" Linda joined in reading from Billy's notes, "—observation room."

They froze. "They're in the same location," the girls said together. Then they both began to read aloud. "I turned to see Billy," read Mary at the exact same time Linda read, "I turned to see Suzy."

Billy and Suzy spoke to each other in short hand.

"The old surgeon?"

"The French nurse?"

"Your mom was the patient."

"Your dad taught a class."

Linda must have read ahead. "Your mom's head became planet earth?!"

"The Earth-Mother," said Sonni.

"Gaia," said Lisa.

The four girls considered Billy and Suzy with a whole new respect. "Do you see their aura?" asked Mary.

"All the colors of the sunset," said Lisa.

"All the colors of the sunrise," said Sonni.

Linda read the last part of Billy's notes. "What's this about Gaia turning red?"

"I never wrote anything about Gaia," said Billy.

"She didn't turn red," said Suzy. "The old doctor said she was, though."

"And that it was scary," said Billy.

"What's *E Pluribus Unum?*" asked Mary. She pointed to the words on Suzy's notes.

"It means, 'From many, one,'" said Suzy.

"What does that mean?" asked Sonni.

Linda said, "The guy in the dream says we have to ask our history teacher."

"You won't, will you?" asked Suzy. She and Billy had American History with the Coven later in the day, and if there was one thing they both had had enough of in their lives, it was the kind of humiliation the Coven could bring with ammunition like this.

"Are you kidding?" asked Linda.

"This is magic," said Mary.

"Powerful magic," said Lisa.

"We have to ask," said Sonni.

"ANY QUESTIONS about last night's homework?"

It was early in the school year, and Billy and Suzy were new to Ms. Fuller's American History class, which meant they lived in fear of her intensity. She was a disciplinarian of the first order, who handed out "zeroes" at the drop of a hat — together with a little math lesson about what a zero would do to bring down a grade point average. If she taught science or algebra, or anything but history — or maybe English — neither Billy nor Suzy would have been so afraid, but their prodigal gifts for the sciences did not extend to something as nebulous as the actions of irrational humans over the centuries.

In Ms. Fuller's class, the kids who skipped two grades

to become the state's youngest high school students were just like their classmates, only more likely to have done their homework.

The Coven, on the other hand, were seniors. They had taken other classes with Ms. Fuller and knew that her hardball exterior was an act. Once students bowed to her discipline and worked to meet her high standards, Ms. Fuller became more than a teacher. She was a mentor, a confidant, and an inspiration.

Linda raised her hand.

Ms. Fuller made a note in her grade book. Participation in discussions was always rewarded. "Linda?"

"It's not exactly about the homework, but I have a question."

Billy saw Ms. Fuller throw a quick glance to the camera in the back of the room. He and Suzy noticed all of their teachers had attitudes about the new cameras. Students and teachers alike had been told they were there for their own good, but most teachers didn't seem to like them. After the conversation Billy and Suzy overheard at Suzy's house, the kids had a better understanding of why. "Does it concern American History?" asked Ms. Fuller.

"I don't know, but someone said I should ask you."

She tossed up her hands. "All right then, ask away."

Linda took a second to figure out how she wanted to phrase this, while Billy and Suzy sank in their chairs, hoping to be left out of it. "If someone said the world," she started, "or maybe, another person, was…" she made air quotes, "'turning red' and that was 'scary,' what would that mean?"

"And, 'I miss E Plural You Dem,'" Mary blurted out.

Ms. Fuller's powerful gaze moved to Mary. "Do you mean *E Pluribus Unum*?"

"Yeah, that," said Mary.

"If you're going to blurt something out in my class, make sure you don't embarrass yourself at the same time."

"Yes, ma'am."

Ms. Fuller's eyes flicked back to the camera, then to Linda. "Your question does have something to do with American history. 'Turning red,' together with 'scare' and *E Pluribus Unum* all point to the Red Scare."

"What's that?" asked Linda.

Ms. Fuller pulled one leg up under the other in her tall chair. She used a drafting table as a desk, so the chair gave her a high perch to keep an eye on her students. "That's a long story — and, by the way, a good subject for an extra credit report for anyone who wants to wipe out a zero or two."

From the downward glances of the class, she didn't have any takers, so she continued. "During World War I, and again after World War II, Americans were crippled by the fear that Russian Communists were planning a Socialist Revolution in the United States. Politicians ran on campaigns of...," she took a slightly sarcastic tone, "'Protecting America from Red Communists.' When they got into office, the steps they took to protect America from what was mostly an imagined threat, did more harm to the country than good."

"What about *E Pluribus Unum*?" Billy surprised himself by asking the question out loud. He was more used to answering questions than asking them.

"It means…" started Ms. Fuller.

"From many, one," said Billy and Suzy together.

"Very good," said Ms. Fuller. She made notes in her grade book. Discussions like these were a big part of her overall grading system. She then pointed to Mary, "That's the way to interrupt a discussion." Back to Billy, she asked, "What else do you know about the saying?"

"It's on the Seal of the United States." He'd Googled it while he wrote the notes from his dream the night before. "And for a long time it was considered the country's motto until 'In God We Trust' was officially voted in."

"Are you reading from your cell phone?" asked Ms. Fuller. She had a keen ear for Wikipedia.

"No," said Billy. "I, uh… I read about it last night."

Ms. Fuller looked to Linda. "I think I might have a conspiracy going on in my class." Her tone as jovial as Billy had ever heard her. Linda smiled and turned up her hands. It was obvious she knew Ms. Fuller would never be mad with students seeking knowledge.

"Billy, when was 'In God we trust' voted into law?"

He sat slack-jawed.

"In 1956," she continued. "The Russian Revolution in 1917, which led to Communism, was as much against the Russian Orthodox Church as it was against the Czar, so they took the Separation of Church and State a lot further than America ever did."

Some of the class started to drift away, but Ms. Fuller was on a roll. If any of the kids bothered to check the Library of Congress, they would find her Master's Thesis, *On Oppression In Modern America*. She loved this stuff. "American Anti-Communists took to calling Russians

'Godless,' so voting 'In God We Trust' as the nation's motto was seen as a stand against the enemy." Once a-gain, Billy noticed her eyes went to the camera in the back of the room, and her tone went back to a forced business-as-usual. "Did that answer your question, Linda?"

"I guess." She had lost her enthusiasm somewhere around the Russian Revolution. "I was hoping it would have something to do with magic."

"Well," said Ms. Fuller, "in a way it does. These mass hysterias, in which the fear of an enemy does more harm to a population than the actual enemy ever could, have happened many times in world history, most often in the Middle Ages, which is where they get their name." She paused for effect, then said straight to the security camera, "They're called 'Witch Hunts.'"

"OKAY, LET'S SUM UP what we know so far."

They'd walked past Suzy's house toward Billy's trailer park. Suzy didn't care. As much as she loved having her dad home, he had been in a grumpy mood most of the time, so hanging out at her place hadn't been as much fun as it used to be. Besides, they had a mystery to solve.

Whenever their walks home led to such heated discussions, it was standard operating procedure to stop at Billy's place, dump their books on the porch, then head to the trailer park's playground. No one ever went there, so it was the perfect place to hang out and solve the world's problems. That was the unspoken plan as they headed down the field across from the trailer park.

"First," said Billy, "you and I are sharing dreams."

He helped Suzy over a gully.

"Always with a black cat that sometimes turns into a French girl." Suzy knew he always helped her over that gully, even though she could probably jump it better than he could. A part of her wondered why she hadn't said anything about it before. Clearly, this wasn't the time to bring it up.

"Or a French girl that sometimes turns into a black cat," said Billy. He added, "And an old man."

"I never dreamed about an old man," said Suzy. "Not without you in my dream."

"Okay, next—"

Suzy's head popped up with the energy of a new idea. "Do you think he could represent your missing father?"

Billy's tone went dark. "We're not interpreting now. We're summing up."

"Fine." Suzy never thought it was fine when he avoided that subject, but he always did. She moved on. "What else?"

"Just with us, or anything?"

"Anything, we're brainstorming. Make a list."

Billy knew she meant a verbal one. "I've been forgetting stuff," said Billy. "Like lapses in time."

"The way the teachers have been acting lately seems funny."

As they got closer to Billy's trailer home they could hear a commotion coming from inside. Billy tried to ignore it. "The Wiccans' spell seemed to have worked."

"Yeah, that was weird."

Peter busted out of the front door. "Billy! Did you take out the trash this morning?"

"Yeah. It stank. What's the problem?"

"The problem is, brat, that you didn't let Mom check it first." So that's what the ruckus was inside. Billy's mother was upset about her treasures. "Now she's blaming me," said Peter, "and I can't get her to take her meds."

"That's not my fault!"

Their mother, face red with tears, barreled out of the front door, nearly knocking Peter off his feet. "Why can't you two get along like you used to?"

Peter answered. "When did the dork and I ever get along?"

"Yeah, Mom, really."

"When you were working on Billy's project, you did."

"What project are you talking about, Mom?" asked Billy.

"I don't know." She seemed to have forgotten why she was so upset and started to go inside. "Whatever that thing was Peter was building for you." She talked to herself all the way into the kitchen. Billy could make out a few more I don't knows and You never tell me anythings.

Peter gave her a minute to fade away, then, "You coming in?"

"Are you leaving?"

"Not for an hour or two."

Billy didn't say anything but took Suzy's book bag and put it with his on the porch. As they walked away, Peter said, "I'll leave a note about her meds."

Billy waved without turning around.

As they walked, Suzy did all of the talking about the mystery they had afoot, but she knew Billy wasn't listening. After a fruitless brainstorming session on the playground, he walked her home without saying a word. At her front door, she couldn't resist.

"Sweet dreams."

BILLY AND SUZY WERE climbing a mountain. Billy had no clue how he got there, so he asked. "How did we get here?"

"I don't know," she said. "I just showed up. Keep going."

The terrain was steep and rocky. The jagged edges of the black rocks cut their fingers, hands, and arms. After helping each other to a ledge, Billy stopped. "If this is a dream, why are we climbing? Why don't we fly?"

"Okay." Suzy jumped off the cliff, immediately falling to what Billy was sure to be her death. But when he look-ed for her over the edge, she swooped past him, sailing up the mountain. "Good idea!"

Billy jumped up after her, but couldn't fly. He jumped again. Nothing. "Why can't I fly?"

"You have to get a running start and build up some speed," said Suzy, who circled overhead like a hawk.

Billy didn't have much room to run, but he gave it a shot — running from the ledge toward the cliff. He jumped, but instead of flying, he slammed into the mountain face.

"No, silly. The other way."

Billy knew what she meant. He had to jump off the cliff. What if he didn't fly? What if this wasn't a dream? What if he'd had a memory lapse like the one that got him in trouble at Oakridge, or when he cleaned up the house without knowing it? What if he really was on a cliff with Suzy and ... Wait a minute! He gazed up at Suzy flying with the ease of a bird. Suzy is flying, he thought. This has to be a dream.

"What are you waiting for?"

Billy took a deep breath, hoped it wasn't his last, and ran off the cliff.

The mountain rushed beside him. Below, razor-sharp shards of rock promised a painful death if Billy didn't learn to fly in the next few milliseconds. He spread his arms, caught the breeze, and lifted his head to take flight just in time to pull up and away from the ground below.

While Suzy flew high above the mountain, Billy liked to stay close to the surface to feel his awesome speed. "I love this!"

"I know," said Suzy. "There is nothing better in the world than flying. I don't know why we don't go to school this way."

"I know. We should."

Part of each of them knew they weren't really flying, and that they could never do this in real life — but it was a small part. The exhilaration and pure joy of flight made them not want to think at all.

Then something caught Suzy's eye. She hung in the air like a cartoon superhero. "Billy, come here."

Effortlessly, Billy joined her and followed her gaze. Beneath them, at the top of the mountain, an old man sat at the mouth of a cave. "That's the surgeon from the operating room," said Suzy.

Billy thought he was familiar from somewhere else, too, but he couldn't put his finger on it.

"Let's go talk to him," said Suzy.

Before Billy could protest, she kicked into a nosedive. Billy followed. Soon they both landed at the old man's feet.

"That climb is supposed to be a struggle," he said without so much as a hello. "You must climb it to earn the wisdom you seek."

"We gained enough wisdom to know that flying is a lot easier," said Suzy.

"Well, then you're doing better than most." The Wise Old Man stood up and waved them toward his cave — which was now a beautiful 1950s-style glass and steel home with an amazing view. "Come on in. Are you hungry?"

"Aren't you guru guys supposed to sleep in the dirt and go starving all the time?" Billy asked.

"Why is it wise men must always starve? If they are so wise, why don't they make themselves more comfortable?"

The next thing Billy and Suzy knew, they were sipping hot chocolate on the balcony of the cliff-top estate. "Why are we here?" asked Suzy.

"Sorry," said the Old Man, who now wore a Nehru jacket and a necklace of large brownish-red beads.

Billy had no idea what a Nehru jacket was, but he thought it made the old guy look more familiar.

The Old Man took a sip of what smelled like steaming orange tea from his cup "I skipped over the part where you tell me everything that's been happening lately. I know that already, and communicating in dreams this way can be so tedious."

"So what should we do?" asked Suzy.

"About what?" asked the man.

Suzy looked at Billy, who looked as uncertain as she felt. "I don't know. About whatever we were telling you about."

"You said the world has all gone crazy."

"Yeah, it kind of feels that way," said Billy.

"Well…" He sipped more tea. "If everyone in the world is crazy, who should you go to for a sane answer?"

ANSWER TO WHAT?

That was the text from Suzy that Billy woke up to in the middle of the night. She'd sent it seconds before, though Billy thought he'd been asleep for hours after the dream. He tried to figure out what the question might be, and who he was supposed to ask, but soon found himself in Dr. Weston's office.

Except it wasn't exactly her office. It was her furniture but the walls, floor, and ceiling were made of ice. She was talking to a patient who Billy couldn't quite see, except that he was a man. His slicked-back hair showed gray under a bad black dye job. He wore a red crushed-velvet suit, emerald rings, and a gold necklace that clashed with his fake-tanned skin. Neither of them noticed Billy.

"What do you mean it's not cold in here?" asked Dr. Weston of the man. "It's literally freezing."

"I've been called cold," said the man, "As a matter of fact, I am the cold." His smiling face suddenly appeared nose-to-nose with Billy's.

Billy stood frozen not with cold, but fear. He knew who the man was.

"He was Evil."

After confirming that they'd shared the same dream the night before, Suzy became more interested in the dream she'd missed, which Billy told her about on their morning walk to school. "How do you know he was evil?" she asked.

"Because, I'd seen him in my other dream."

"Oh, yeah. I forgot about that one." Suzy was stumped. "What does your doctor say?"

"She says dreams use metaphors sometimes."

"Duh!"

"She doesn't like to get into dream analysis."

"So let's not, either," said Suzy. "We have two riddles to solve."

"Riddles?"

"Yes. 'In a crazy world, who do you turn to for sane answers?' and … I don't know. What did the evil guy say?"

"Not an evil guy. He is Evil with a capital E."

"Fine, what did Evil say?"

"He said he was the cold."

"So there's our second riddle," said Suzy. "How can Evil be cold?" Satisfied that she'd interpreted this correctly, Suzy picked up her pace.

Billy was left standing. "I don't think that's the right riddle."

"WHO ASKED, 'IN a crazy world, who do you turn to for sane answers'?"

Billy took a chance during the discussion period of history. He figured Ms. Fuller had the answer before, so why wouldn't she have it again?

Puzzlement ran across Ms. Fuller's face. "I don't think I've ever heard that quote, Billy. What's it in reference to?"

Billy didn't want to say he heard it in a dream with Suzy last night, and was saved from that humiliation by a knock on the door. A man who Billy didn't recognize stared through the window; his face seemed incapable of laughter. Ms. Fuller saw who it was and held up her index finger to the man meaning, "Wait until I acknowledge you." She turned back to Billy. "Well?"

"It's okay, if you have to go."

"He can wait until this class is over. You are more important than anything that man has to say."

Ms. Fuller's harsh tone took the class a bit by surprise. Some sat up in their seats, looking to each other with an unspoken did-you-hear-what-I-heard expression. Others tried to see who "that man" was.

"Billy, you were asking about a crazy world," said Ms. Fuller, "well remember this — all of you." She always had her class's attention, but this was intense. No one flinched when the door to the class opened and the serious man came in uninvited. "Kids, history happens every moment. You are a part of it. It is happening all around you, and Billy — right now it is a very crazy world."

"Mrs. Fuller," said the man, who obviously hadn't heard her preference to be called "Ms."

"I am *teaching!*"

"Not anymore," said the man. He took a paper out

of his pocket that must have been important.

Ms. Fuller ignored him. "Billy, I hope you find the answer to your question."

The man was insistent. "Mrs. Fuller!"

She closed her books. "Because we could all use some answers right now."

She took her things and left the room. A young, professionally dressed woman came in with a sparklingly new history textbook.

"Kids," said the serious man, "this is your new history teacher." He pointed up at the security camera. "I trust we won't have any problems making this transition."

"BILLY, YOU HAVE to do something!"

It wasn't Suzy making this plea, but the whole class, including Linda Lubinski and the rest of the Coven. They surrounded Billy in the hall after the bell as if he were a sacred cauldron.

"Why don't you come up with a spell?" asked Billy. "It worked on me, didn't it?"

"Oh, we are," said Linda.

"Several spells," said Mary.

"But this is big," said Lisa.

"We're going to need help," said Sonni.

"Why me?" asked Billy — not that he didn't appreciate the attention from the funky-beautiful seniors.

"Oh, come on, Billy," said Linda.

"Everyone knows you have Principal Dillon wrapped around your finger," said Mary.

There was an odd pause while Billy and Suzy waited for Lisa and Sonni to speak up. When they didn't, Suzy did. "Billy, they're right. You have to speak to Dillon."

"You go with him," said Linda. "Get Ms. Fuller back. We can't go through our senior year without her."

"MR. DILLON!"

Billy charged into the office like he owned the place. Suzy, the Coven, and Ms. Fuller's entire history class followed him.

"Not now, Billy." For the first time in their relationship, Mr. Dillon sounded like he meant business.

Billy stammered, so Suzy stepped in, "No, now, Mr. Dillon. We deserve the right to know what's going on."

Just then, the serious man from class led Ms. Fuller out of Dillon's office. "We'll deal with her downtown," he told Dillon.

Tears ran down Ms. Fuller's face, but she held her head high for her kids. "Fight, kids! Fight this with all your might."

"These *children* should be in class," the man said.

"Yes," shouted Linda, "with our *teacher!*" She had tears on her face, too, but her proclamation earned cheers from all her classmates. The serious man took Ms. Fuller by the arm and pushed her out of the office.

"Mr. Dillon," said Billy, "do something."

Mr. Dillon flicked his eyes to the security camera in the office. He then smiled, put his arms around Billy and Suzy, and escorted them out of the office. This move put their backs to the camera. "They're watching," Dillon said quietly through his smile. "They are always watching."

Five

MOTHER KNOWS BEST

"BILLY? SUZY? Can we have a word?"

Mr. Dillon and his wife drove slowly up to the kids. They had followed them on their walk home. The minute they were out of sight from any prying eyes, the couple pulled up next to them. This was extremely out of the ordinary, even for Dillon, who was dependent on Billy for keeping the school's computers up and running.

"Ah…" Billy wordlessly questioned Suzy. She gave a "why not?" shrug of her shoulders. "Yeah, okay," said Billy.

Dillon got out of the car to walk with the kids. His wife, who was also his secretary, drove alongside. "You kids know there is a new Federal School Board, right?"

"The one that replaced all of our textbooks with the crappy ones?" asked Suzy.

"That's the one," said Dillon. He stared off into the distance.

"Everything went crazy over the summer. People became obsessed with the schools. What was supposed to be a minimum standard is now the only one," said Dillon. "Any teacher like Ms. Fuller who refuses to lower the bar, who teaches more than the basics — and never mind that every year she got all of her students over the high goals she'd set. That doesn't matter to them." Dillon was rambling. "They would rather have all the kids be mindless drones than to have their minds turned on."

"Is that why Ms. Fuller was fired?" asked Billy.

"Yes, and that's why there are cameras in the rooms. At first they were to provide security. At least that's what they told us. It wasn't long before they were being used to monitor the teachers."

"That's why the teachers all give them funny looks," said Billy.

"It is," said Dillon. They took a few steps in awkward silence before he got to the point. "The reason I wanted to talk to you both is ... well, I'm not sure exactly. I suppose I wanted you to know that we don't like it any more than you do, but these are our jobs. We can't fight it."

"Are you saying we should?" asked Suzy.

"No, I didn't mean that." Dillon started to continue that line of thought, then he got a cockeyed look on his face and to himself said, "Huh," Then to the kids, "I mean, officially, no. I'm not saying that you kids should do something ... officially, I'm not saying that." He started back to his car. "Even if it is a good idea."

"Thanks, Mr. Dillon," said Suzy.

"It's a crazy world, kids."

Billy and Suzy had the same thought. Suzy spoke up. "Mr. Dillon, in a crazy world, who do you think we should turn to for sane answers?"

"I don't know," said Dillon. "A crazy person?" He got in the car and they drove away.

Suzy didn't want to say it, so Billy did. "My mom!" He started running toward the trailer park. "Come on!"

BILLY AND SUZY FOUND his mother in the front yard of the trailer home with a broom shooing away unseen little beasts. "They're gathering, Billy! Come inside the dome." She pulled them into the yard, then gave the neighbor's yard gnomes a hard stare. "I don't know how much longer your force field is going to hold up."

Billy explained to Suzy. "She thinks I made some kind of invisible force field to keep the gnomes out of the yard."

Peter came storming out of the house carrying two pills and a small bottle of water. "Where have you been? She's still off her meds, and you know I have to get to work. I can't stay around here watching her all day."

Billy snapped back. "How was I supposed to know she was flipping out again? Did you text me?"

"Would you have read it?"

"No."

"Then why ask?"

Their arguing was typical, but for some reason it got more of a reaction from their mother than usual. "Will you two quit arguing? You're doing exactly what they want!" She was so upset she slobbered like an old hound dog. "You need to get along like you did before. They don't like it when people get along. It makes them weak."

"Mom," said Billy, "I told you before, we've never gotten along."

"Yes, you have. You did when you were working together."

Peter corrected her this time. "Mom, you're nuts. Please take your meds."

"I will if you two will be civil."

"Okay," said Peter. "We'll make nice, I promise. Now take them." He handed his mother her pills and the water. She took her pills, then opened her mouth for Peter to confirm she wasn't faking it.

"Finally," said Peter. To Billy he said, "Do you have her? Can I go to work?"

"Yes," said Billy.

"Fine." Peter got into his car and drove off with squealing wheels.

"Mrs. Bobble?" Suzy approached her slowly, as if she were trying to catch a feral cat. "What were they working on together?"

Billy answered. "Nothing, Suzy. She's making things up."

"Billy, the world is crazy. Maybe she's not."

"You worked on it, too," said Billy's mother. "You all three did."

"What was it, Mrs. Bobble?"

"I don't know," she said, "but I can show you."

"Please," said Suzy.

Billy's mom handed him her broom. "Guard the door." She didn't wait for a response but headed toward Peter's makeshift garage. Suzy followed.

Billy eyed the yard gnomes, who did seem to be

gathered around the edge of their yard in a wide arch. He then caught himself having stupid thoughts, rolled his eyes and said, "Ridiculous." He threw down the broom and took off after his mother and Suzy. "You'd better not touch anything in Peter's garage. He'll kill all of us."

Mrs. Bobble rummaged around under the blue tarp that was stretched over a two-by-four frame attached to the side of the trailer home. Here in his "garage," Peter worked on his Dodge Charger — and now that he had a job as a mechanic, any other car that might need work off the books. The place was immaculate. His high-end tool cabinets — all bought second-hand — were locked and chained to a concrete slab that he'd poured to make a smooth floor suitable for driving. The only thing unsecured was a forgotten set of old school lockers that Peter had started out with years ago. They were now shoved in a corner growing rust. Mrs. Bobble headed toward the lockers.

"It's in here," she said.

"Mom, there's nothing in there," said Billy. "Nothing real, I mean."

"You'll see," she said. She had trouble opening the locker, so Suzy helped.

When it opened, out fell a dozen wooden novelty magic wands, each one split down the middle with the insides carved out in a groove.

"See Mom, it's just..." Before he could finish, Suzy picked one up. She slowly turned to Billy. They were both in shock.

"I remember," said Billy.

Suzy recalled for the first time in months what she'd

told the police in the spring. "Billy Bobble made a magic wand."

SUZY GRABBED BILLY by the shoulders. "You had the idea!"

He grabbed hers back. "You thought of DNA!" They were both giddy with the flood of memories. "And the Old Man," said Billy. "The Teacher."

"And Fame, your familiar."

"She's the cat from our dreams." They said that together.

"That explains the Coven's magic trick on my calculus test."

"Sometimes we forget things," said Billy's mother. "Sometimes we need a reminder to spark our memories."

"I remember everything," said Billy. "The idea to make real magic."

"Because Stockwell nearly killed you in front of everyone in the courtyard at lunch?" Suzy added.

"What? Oh, yeah, whatever," said Billy. "I remember the explosion in your basement."

"And at school."

"Mom!" said Billy as another memory washed through his brain. "I really did create a force field to keep out the gnomes."

"I told you so, honey. There's nothing my Billy can't do."

Suzy then recalled. "You saved those soldiers."

Billy's mood dropped. "Yeah. And people died."

Suzy's thoughts still spun with new memories. One of them was how upset Billy was about the deaths of the terrorists he'd brought back from Kashmir. "That wasn't your fault, Billy."

"But I gave them the wand."

Suzy recalled Billy throwing his wand away. "Yeah, okay, that part was your fault." She gave Billy a friendly whack on the shoulder. Billy smiled enough to show that her gallows humor lightened his mood a bit. "Billy, they're clever. The Teacher told you that. They've even fooled him over the centuries."

"Whoever 'they' are."

"They must have messed with our memory."

"Not just ours, and not just memory." Billy thought of his first psychiatric visit. "Didn't your mom say there was a psychiatrist at the police station?"

"My memory isn't that good without being cursed." Suzy held up a finger. "Wait." Billy could almost see images flash in her eyes as she reacted to her sudden total recall. "Yes, she did."

"The only person that could be is my doctor, and she didn't know you at all. And there was nothing in my record about the explosion at school."

"You know what I think?" asked Suzy, clearly ready to answer her own question. "I think 'they' are the ones responsible for the world going crazy, for us losing our memories, and the witch hunts."

Billy pulsed with a sudden realization. "It wasn't a dream."

"What?"

"The Teacher was in my room just as I woke up. He

said that only I could solve the world's problems."

Suzy crossed her arms, looked over her glasses at Billy and said, "And you were going to tell me this, when?" Her tone left no doubt that she was displeased.

"I thought I did."

"Nope."

"Sorry." She didn't give any indication that his apology was accepted, so Billy moved ahead. "Can we get on with saving the world?"

Suzy relaxed. "We should talk to my dad."

"Yeah."

Billy's mom stepped into the conversation. "Does this mean you and Peter will start getting along?"

"Oh. Mom," said Billy to himself. To Suzy he said, "I can't go. I have to keep an eye on her."

"You run along, Billy," said his mother. "I'll go next door to have a chat with Martha. My meds have kicked in, so I'm fine."

"Are you sure?"

She smiled. "I'm sure."

"Okay, then. Suzy, let's go!"

They rushed to the porch to get Suzy's books, but Billy stopped short. He ran back and gave his mother, the woman who had caused him so much embarrassment in his life, a great big hug. "Thanks, Mom," he whispered. "You're the best."

"HUMPH."

That's all General Quinofski said after Billy and Suzy raced through the whole story. They had barged into his home office, out of breath and excited. Their presentation was more a vomiting of words than a recollection of evidence.

"You don't believe us," said Suzy.

"I didn't say that."

"You don't have to, Dad, it's written all over your face."

"Billy," said General Quinofski, "why don't you let me have one of my people run you home?"

"He doesn't need to go home, Dad."

"I can get home by myself," said Billy. He recognized the tone in the General's voice. It was the 'I need to talk about you behind your back' tone that parents often use when they want the kids out of the room. "Run along and play," they would say. Billy used to fight it, but between doctors talking to Peter about their mom's condition and teachers talking to each other about school politics, Billy had learned to let it be. Still, the Quinofskis felt as close to him as family, so this stung a bit.

General Quinofski picked up the phone on his desk and pressed a button. "No, Billy, I insist. You can meet the driver outside if you like." Then he spoke into the phone. "Yes, I need a driver to pick up Billy Bobble from my residence."

"Fine," Billy said to the General, and "See you tomorrow," to Suzy before he left the office. He was halfway out of the front door when he remembered that they hadn't talked about Ms. Fuller's situation. He doubled back to remind Suzy, but before he got to the office he heard her father.

"Whose idea was this?" He had his stern parent voice on.

"What do you mean?"

"I mean…" He paused and took in a deep breath.

"You think we're lying."

"Lying? No," he said without a spec of doubt in his voice. "I know you both better than that."

"Then what is it?"

"Memories can be a tricky thing, Suzy. So can delusions."

"You think we're delusional?"

"Not you, Suzy."

Outside the door Billy knew what was coming. He didn't have to hear the words, but he did, and they hurt. "Billy's family has a history of mental—"

"Dad, that's not what this is!"

Billy hated that she had to defend him, but he didn't have the courage to bust in there and state his case. Besides, the General might be right.

"Suzy, listen to what you're asking me to believe — that people's memories have been erased, mine included; that school records have been changed; that police records have been changed, and that no one knows about it but you, Billy, and his schizophrenic mother? How is all of this supposed to have happened?"

"We told you, Dad, by…" She couldn't finish her sentence. She knew it wouldn't help her case.

Her father finished it for her. "Magic?"

There was a long silence. For a second Billy thought he might get caught eavesdropping. Then the General said, "I'm going to have to talk to your mother about this."

"Fine," said Suzy. "Ask her where we got the silverware."

"The what?"

"Exactly."

"Don't get smart with me, young lady."

Too late, thought Billy. She's already smarter than most.

"Until I have a chance to talk with your mother, I don't want you talking to Billy."

"But Dad!"

"I mean it. No phones. No texts. No computers. No communication technology of any kind, do you understand me?"

"Yes, sir," said Suzy.

Billy slipped out of the front door to catch his ride, but he knew what Suzy wasn't saying: Dreams aren't technology.

"MY DAD'S an idiot."

They were dreaming.

"No he's not."

It was night in the playground. No sign of old men, cats, French girls, or Evil, almost as if this was a normal late night walk. Billy sat in a swing, his gangly legs folded under him. His head hung down.

Suzy paced. She was a bundle of energy. "Billy, you are not crazy."

"Really? We're talking in a dream. I believe that we invented a magic wand, saved a bunch of captured Special Forces soldiers, and those with any knowledge of that have had their memory wiped, along with school records and police reports. Plus, I have a strong suspicion that evil beings from the Quantum World are manipulating politicians to try to control our schools and military. Does that sound sane?"

"It sounds like the truth to me."

"Maybe your father's right. You've bought into the same delusions I have."

"Billy, that's ridiculous."

"Why?"

"Because we have witnesses. For the dreams, I mean."

Billy stared at the dirt.

"Billy?"

He ignored her and asked the night air a question. "Why is this dream so normal?"

"I don't know, Billy, I don't care. What are we going to do?"

Billy twisted in the swing. His mind churned. "We think we made a magic wand, right?"

"We did. Well, you did. I just thought of the DNA part."

"And that was a big part of it, wasn't it?" Billy stopped twisting. "If it was real."

"It was real, Billy. I know it was real."

"That's exactly what my delusion of you would say."

"Billy, what do I have to do to convince you that the wand was real?"

He finally raised his head, caught her eye, and smiled. "Make another one."

Six

K.I.P.

T HEY SPENT AN AGE without talking. Suzy had promised her Dad that she wouldn't communicate with Billy until he'd had a chance to talk it over with her mother, so she didn't. One day in study hall she gave him a cotton swab and a plastic sandwich bag. Without a word, Billy swabbed his cheek, sealed the stick in the bag, and gave it back. A week later, she showed him a long thin glass tube. It was his DNA, separated. The introns — sequences common to every living thing we know of — looped out and back along the length of the tube. The tiny bit of DNA unique to Billy curled up in the bulb at one end. It was separate but still connected. Sort of like Billy and Suzy.

That night, Billy snuck Peter's split wands out of the old locker and into his book bag. At school, he gave them to Suzy. The day after that, she returned one of them wrapped in tape. Billy knew the DNA was inside, and that he'd have to be careful not to screw it up.

A week earlier, Suzy had talked her mother into putting their old scanner-printer-fax machine out on the curb for a junk collector to pick up. That collector was Billy. To construct his first wand, he had made the machine into a Kirlian camera. With his DNA inside the wooden wand, he wrapped it in tiny copper wires from an old toy's electric motor. With the Kirlian camera, he checked the electromagnetic field, manipulated the wires, checked it again, and repeated the process until he knew that, once a current passed through the wires, a perfect implosion field would push the introns out of his dimension and put the owner of the DNA into the Quantum World.

"It didn't work," were the first words Billy said to Suzy after she informed him that the ban had been lifted — at least as far as school was concerned. They were on their way to study hall.

"Why not?"

"I don't know," he said, then offered another question. "Why haven't we been dreaming?"

The answer would have to wait, as Linda and the Wiccans actually started a conversation with Suzy and Billy right when they walked in the door. "We want to start a protest!" they said together.

Linda grabbed the front of her desk and leaned forward like a little kid. "I'm more excited about this than anything in my life."

Suzy asked Billy, "Do you remember when…?"

"Yes."

"Do you think this is…?"

"I'm not sure," said Billy.

They were talking about the time the Wiccans were susceptible to the dark forces of the Quantum world. Apparently, their minds could be easily influenced by evil. Billy had been told by the Teacher that there were no coincidences, not where he was concerned, and that he should be careful about people who seemed suddenly compelled to do something out of character. He listened with a cautious ear.

"We want to protest more than Ms. Fuller's firing. We want to cover the whole textbook thing and everything," said Linda.

"We want kids all over the country to join us," said Mary.

"To start protests of their own," said Lisa.

"Make it a national movement," said Sonni.

Then it was Linda's turn. "We were thinking. Your dreams about the Red Scare and the witch hunts that Ms. Fuller talked about are what got all of this started."

"We told you that was powerful magic," said Mary.

"The thing is," said Lisa, "we don't know much about that. Protests, I mean."

"And our textbooks are crap," said Sonni.

"And the Internet is just too much," said Lisa.

Linda took it from there. "We were wondering — I mean, we know history isn't your best subject and all — but we need help learning about this stuff."

"Normally, we'd ask Ms. Fuller," said Mary.

"She'd give us extra credit," said Lisa.

"You guys didn't get to know her all that well," said Sonni, "but she really meant a lot to us."

Billy couldn't figure out where he stood with this idea. It seemed like a good one, but the dark beings of the Quantum World work in mysterious ways. Best to keep arm's distance. Besides that, he and Suzy had weightier problems to deal with. "We'd like to help," said Billy, "but we … will be helping in other ways."

Suzy was on the same page. "And Billy and I don't know anything about starting protests so…"

Her trailing thought was interrupted when an unrecognized voice cut through the room. "Girls!"

Everyone checked the doors to the classroom, expecting to see someone from the office barging in with a message, but no one was there.

"You'll need a hall pass." It was Mrs. Nelson, the teacher who hardly ever said anything in the two years Billy and Suzy had had her for study hall. "Billy, will you be going with them?"

"Uh…?" Billy had no idea what she was talking about.

"To the library to help them with their research."

The kids were dumbfounded. Mrs. Nelson could hear!

She picked up on their surprise. "In times like these," she said, tapping her finger near her ear, "it's best to keep one's wits about them." In one small gesture, Mrs. Nelson almost confirmed the rumor that she'd turn down her hearing aid during study hall. She certainly indicated she knew about it. "Billy? Are you going with them?"

"Yeah, sure."

The Witches of Winston High, Billy, and Suzy walked up to Mrs. Nelson's desk to get the hall pass she was writing. In the lower right-hand corner, she wrote a small K.I.P. "Show Mrs. Maltin this." With her pencil she subtly tapped on the inscription to make sure the kids saw it. "She'll help you with anything you need."

Suzy spoke as if this wasn't as strange as it was. "Will do, Mrs. Nelson."

Mary was the first one to talk once they were in the hall. "Was that friggin' strange? It was friggin' strange, right?"

"Shh!" said Linda and Suzy together. Then Linda asked, "What should we do?"

Suzy said, "We can't talk here."

Billy came up with an answer no one would have thought he'd say in a million years. "Let's get stoned." He walked toward an exit, leaving five shocked young women in his wake.

"BILLY? YOU get high?"

Billy led them outside toward the back of the gym. Along the way he answered Linda's question. "Of course not! I have no extra brain cells to throw away. Don't be stupid."

Suzy picked up on the questioning. "Then what were you talking about back there?"

"Stoner's row," he said, as they arrived at the back of the gym. "No security cameras. We can talk freely back here."

Mary's turn for a question. "How did you know about this place?"

"I nearly got killed here last year." Billy's voice was calm considering the admission. "Long story. Anyway, I checked this out on the first day of school, and sure enough, they didn't put cameras back here."

"Am I crazy," asked Linda, "or did Mrs. Nelson specifically point to—" She cut herself off and grabbed the hall pass from Suzy. "To this. What is this?" She showed them all the K.I.P. on the note. "What does it mean?"

"What are you all doing back here?" Principal Dillon scared the wits out of all of the kids, even Billy.

Suzy stayed sharp. She snatched back the hall pass and showed it to Dillon with her thumb over the K.I.P. "We have a hall pass, sir."

Dillon wasn't impressed. "Yes, that is a hall pass. Halls are on the inside of buildings."

Suzy then moved her thumb. When Dillon saw the K.I.P. his tone became low and serious. "Where were you heading?"

"The library," said Suzy. "We have some research to do."

"Right," said Dillon. "Don't talk too long out here, and have a good excuse for the delay. Mrs. Maltin will need it."

Suzy clarified. "You mean we'll need it for Mrs. Maltin?"

Dillon stared off into space for a second, then made eye contact with Suzy and ever so slightly shook his head. Without another word he walked off.

"WAIT HERE."

By the iron-fisted way she ran her library, no one would have guessed Mrs. Maltin loved her job. Though she could have retired two years earlier, she said they would have to drag her from the bookshelves kicking and screaming. Her reaction to the K.I.P. was subtler than Dillon's. Upon seeing it, she never dropped her stern librarian persona, but led them to a table under one of the security cameras. "Here," was punctuated with a gesture like she was pushing them against the wall. Clearly, she wanted them to stay behind the frame of the camera.

"Remember," she added, "this is a library." She held her index finger to her lips, the international sign for quiet that the kids had seen her do on countless occasions, but this time, as she took her finger away, she subtly pointed up toward the camera.

A minute later, she returned with their American History textbook. Sonni protested. "This is the same crappy textbook we already have."

Mrs. Maltin put the book on the desk. Clearly, another book was stuffed inside. "I think you'll find," she said, "there is more information here than you might think, if you look close enough." She walked away.

Suzy took out the hidden book, *The History and Evolution of Civil Disobedience* by Ann Fuller.

Mary grabbed the book from Suzy. "Ann Fuller? I wonder if she's any relation to Ms. Fuller."

"She is Ms. Fuller," said Suzy.

"How do you know?" asked Mary.

Before Suzy could give a long answer, Linda jumped in. "Her picture's on the back of the book."

Mary had the book open to the introduction. "Who's Edmund Burke? Does he teach here, too?"

Lisa read over her shoulder. "No, he's the guy who said the quote above his name."

Mary read out loud. "'The only thing necessary for the triumph of evil is for good men to do nothing.'"

Linda said, "Yeah? Well, some good women are going to do something." Then she added as an afterthought, "And you, Billy."

Mary was on to another question. "What's civil disobedience?"

"Protests," said Sonni. "The teachers have given us a handbook on how to protest, written by Ms. Fuller herself."

SUZY'S MOM PICKED THEM up from school as part of the great "Billy might be crazy" compromise. Without Suzy, Billy would have to walk around the city-sized military base instead of cutting through, so Mrs. Quinofski agreed to drive Billy home. It wasn't a rule, but both kids figured talk of magic would be off the table. Consequently, nothing much was said at all until they got to Billy's trailer home.

"See ya." Suzy said as Billy stepped out of the car.

"Yeah, see ya," said Billy. His mood was so low he felt like he had to lift it up just to get out of the car.

Suzy's sigh almost brought tears to Mrs. Quinofski's eyes. "Maybe we can have him over for dinner this weekend," she said, as if that were some consolation.

Billy worked on the wand all afternoon and evening. Everything was exactly the same as the first one, but it wasn't working. He wished he could walk over to Suzy's to brainstorm with her about it, but that was exactly what her parents were most afraid of — the storms that Billy's brain might come up with.

By the time his head hit the pillow, Billy was out cold

and before he knew it he was standing in the hall of his trailer home. It was dark, but he could make out the glowing eyes of a black cat at the other end of the hall. To see the rest of her, he turned on the light. When he did, the cat morphed into him and turned the light off via the switch on that end of the hall.

Billy turned the light on again. Other Billy turned it off.

Billy turned it on. Billy turned it off. Repeat.

After several of these clicks, Suzy appeared in the middle of the room. "There are two of you."

"No," said Billy. "That one started out as the cat."

"Yeah," said Billy. "That one started out as the cat."

On. Off. On. Off.

Suzy tightened her fists against her side and closed her eyes. "Will you cut that out!?"

"I would love to," said Billy, "but every time I turn the lights on, he cuts them off."

"Yeah," said Billy. "Every time I turn them on, he cuts them off."

On. Off. On. Off.

"Do you know what the definition of insanity is?" asked Suzy.

"If you mean what Einstein said it was," said Billy.

On.

"Doing the same thing over and over again and expecting a different result."

Off.

"That's not the actual definition."

On.

"It was just Einstein being smart."

Off.

"Yeah, well," said Suzy. "Being smart was pretty much what he did for a living, so I think you should consider it."

On. Off. On. Off.

When Suzy couldn't take it anymore, she walked over to one of the switches and held it in place. The lights were off. "Now flip your switch," she told the Billy down the hall. He did. The lights stayed on. One of the Billy's changed back into a cat.

The other one woke up and sent Suzy a text message. "We're going to need your DNA."

"YOU'RE GOING TO MAKE a wand for me?"

Suzy barely talked above a whisper, even though they were in a hall full of kids changing classes. The school had become a house of whispers. The most repeated one that day was "bring your lunch to third period." Everyone was saying it.

Billy ignored the lunch whispers to answer Suzy's question. "I think having the same DNA in two different wands makes them counteract each other. At least, that's what I got from the dream."

"So you're going to make a wand for me?"

"Yeah, if that's okay."

"Okay? What took you so long?" She reached into her bag and pulled out a shipping tube. "Here's my DNA."

Billy opened the tube to find a wand wrapped in tape. "When did you do this?"

"The same time I did yours," she said. "I figured

you'd get around to making a wand for me sooner or later."

THIRD PERIOD HISTORY CLASS had gone from Billy and Suzy's favorite non-math-or-science class to their least. All Ms. Fuller's replacement did was have them read aloud from the new textbook. Then she would drill the class on a quiz. The next day, she would give them a quiz with the exact same questions she'd brought up the day before. Gone was any discussion time. Gone was the encouragement for free thought. Yes, the zeroes were gone, too — but so were the rewards offered to anyone willing to work for them.

Suzy was almost asleep by the end of class when Linda whispered something to her. "What?" mouthed Suzy.

"When the bell rings," Linda repeated, "stay in your seat."

Suzy didn't have time to pass the message on to Billy before the clanging of the bell erupted through the halls. Billy started to get up, but was immediately overwhelmed by the lack of noise. He was one of only two other students who got up to go to their next class, and he didn't hear the usual cacophony of noise from a thousand or so kids in the halls.

Mrs. Boring Substitute looked cock-eyed at the kids in their seats. "Class is over, you should all move on to your next one."

The students didn't move. Mrs. Boring looked out of the windows to see several news vans pull up. "What is going on?" she asked.

"This is a protest," said Linda.

"A peaceful protest," said Mary.

"But we're serious," said Sonni.

"We have demands," said Lisa.

"Demands?" asked the dullest teacher of the year.

"Yes," said Linda. "As soon as the press sets up, we'll let you know what they are."

Mrs. Boring took a step toward the window, then thought better of whatever she was going to do there. She faced the class again. "I have another class coming in here any minute."

"No you don't," said Linda.

"We cancelled it," said Mary.

"It's a sit-in," said Sonni.

"The whole school is in on it," said Lisa.

Everyone expected Linda to continue the four-voiced conversation, but she just folded her arms and smiled.

Mrs. Boring didn't know what to do. She stepped toward the window again, then the door, then the class. Finally, she said, "I'm going to see Principal Dillon about this." She headed for the exit, but turned around to get her purse. "Remember," she said, "The security cameras are watching you."

When she left, the class heard her say to someone, "What are you doing in the halls? You're not supposed to be in the halls without a pass."

"We're between periods," came a strong male voice. "How do you expect us to get to class if we can't be in the halls?"

Everyone laughed as three senior boys came in. Billy and Suzy only recognized one of them, Charles Su, school president. Called C-Su by his friends, Charles had the charisma of an honest, caring, politician and the brains to lead Winston High's debate team to the state championship for the last three years.

Linda ran up and gave him a high five. "That was great!"

"You guys heard that?" Charles asked the whole class, who nodded heads or said something in the affirmative. "I don't have time to go over the whole thing, okay, so let me give ya'll the quick rundown. Linda and I, and the rest of us—" He meant the Coven and his two other friends, one of whom climbed up on a desk to unplug the room's security camera. "—are the temporary protest committee, okay? We'll elect real officers once we get this sit-in rolling. Does anyone have a problem with that?"

"Not at all," said Suzy, with so much enthusiasm that Billy gave her a look.

"We talked about adding you and Billy, if you're interested," said C-Su.

"Sure," said Suzy.

"Ah, we might have to wait on that," said Billy. "We have another project that will help the cause, but it will take a lot of our time."

"Great," said C-Su. "Let us know if you need any help."

"Sure thing," said Suzy, which earned her a wink from C-Su.

Billy wrestled with a myriad of feelings about C-Su. Part of him didn't like his slick persona or the way Suzy looked at him, another part wanted to be him.

C-Su went on with his briefing. "So you guys know, here are our demands: One, Ms. Fuller gets her job back.

Two, we get our old textbooks back. And three, the security cameras be removed from the classrooms." He paused to gauge the reaction, which was positive. "Now, we probably won't get number three, but it's a negotiation tactic. Our real objective is to have the footage be sealed and only accessible in the investigation of a crime, and then only with a warrant."

"That's smart," said Suzy. She made a mental note that if she ever needed an attorney, or a dinner date, she would call Charles.

THE NEGOTIATIONS STARTED with an on-camera statement by Linda, with the rest of the leaders in the background. They were live on the TV stations with news at noon, so kids with smart phones let everyone crowd around to watch. Billy and Suzy got an invitation to come outside with the team to watch live. "We need your magic," said Linda.

Suzy smacked Billy in the arm when he started to argue the point. "We'd love to," she told Linda, while looking at Charles.

Things went sour when a reporter with a kid at the high school applied her insider knowledge about the Witches of Winston High. "Is it true that you claim to be witches?"

"It's 'Wiccan,' and so what?" said Linda.

Charles stepped in for quick damage control. "I think we can all agree with Justice Hugo Black when he said, 'A union of government and religion tends to destroy government and degrade religion.'" He gave a big smile while he paused for some sort of audience reaction, but only got one response.

"Here! Here!" said Suzy.

"Do you even know what he's talking about?" Billy asked when people stopped looking at her.

"Not a bit," she said, "but it sounded really smart."

"How come when he says something that sounds smart, girls like it, and when I say something that's actually smart, they think I'm a dork?"

"Do you really want an answer?"

"No."

The reporter wouldn't let go of her scoop. "Why should the whole school be held hostage by people who believe in witchcraft?"

"Because," said Linda, "Wiccan is an established religion."

The woman laughed. Charles stepped in front of Linda. "This protest isn't about religion," he said.

"Actually, it is." The cameras whipped around to find out who spoke, and even to her surprise, it was Suzy. She buried her face in Billy's chest. "What did I say?"

"What I wanted to say, but didn't have the guts," he told her. "Go for it."

"Suzy?" asked C-Su. "You have something you'd like to say?" His tone was inviting.

"Ah…"

C-Su stepped aside with a gesture for her to take the stage. "Come on up."

"Okay."

C-Su leaned into the collection of microphones to make a quick introduction. "Suzy Quinofski, everyone."

A murmur went through the handful of reporters.

They all recognized the surname.

Suzy stepped in front of the cameras not knowing what would come out of her mouth — words or her breakfast. Turned out to be words. "Charles is mostly right." She smiled at him. That was a mistake. He smiled back, and she nearly fainted. Quickly she looked back to the press and hoped they took her blushing as being nervous in front of reporters, not Charles. "We don't like these textbooks, not because they are controversial, but because they are not."

Suzy paused to think of what she was going to say next. During that time, her words went into the microphones, through the air to the TV stations, then transmitted back through the Internet and the air once again to be projected out of the phones of all the kids watching inside. A spontaneous "Yes!" could be heard by everyone in and around the building.

The positive response gave Suzy a rush, which put words in her head. "A bland education is a boring education." This time the encouraging cheers came from the committee behind her. "We don't want to be taught how to take a test, but how to write one!

"When you go to a doctor, do you want him or her to believe that an intelligent designer gave you that illness? Or, would you want her to know that it's caused by a virus that evolved from another virus, and that, with the right dosage of anti-viral drugs, you could be cured of something that was incurable a decade before?"

No one could hear it, but they all felt a collective "Huh?" coming from the school.

"My point is," said Suzy, then she corrected herself.

"Our point is, that we are fighting for our education. The education our parents and this community paid for, and that we need to survive in the modern world. There is no 'belief' in education. There is no 'faith' in education. There is no 'spirituality' in education. For those things we turn to our churches, our temples, our covens, our friends and family."

There is a unique kind of silence that falls when a large group of people all stop to listen as one.

"That's why it doesn't matter that Linda and her friends are Wiccan. Sure, I think that's crap as much as you do, but it doesn't make Linda a bad person. It doesn't change what she says up here about education, because she isn't talking about her faith. She's talking about education. There's a difference."

Suzy then realized she may have made Charles's point. Her voice softened. "I think I may have argued myself into a circle."

"Mr. Dillon," asked the same reporter. "Are you going to negotiate with a bunch of kids who believe in witchcraft?"

Suzy's head dropped in defeat. Dillon escorted her back from the microphones. "Nice try," he whispered before turning back to answer the reporter. "I am always available to listen to the grievances of any and all of my students."

Suzy didn't stand with the seniors. Instead, she snuck back over with Billy. "They didn't hear a word I said."

"The reporters didn't," said Billy, "but they did." He nodded his head toward the school. "And they're online."

"NICE SPEECH, HONEY."

No one was being held hostage, so when school was over and the negotiations hadn't finished, Mrs. Quinofski came to pick up Suzy and Billy as per usual.

"Oh, my God, you saw it?" Suzy was mortified before she'd even gotten her seatbelt on.

"I saw it," said Mrs. Q. "Your father saw it. Your grandparents saw it. Pretty much everyone in the country saw it since it was picked up on all the cable news stations."

"Are you mad?" asked Suzy. Then, more importantly, "Is Dad mad?"

Mrs. Q. sighed, then said, "We were a little shocked at first. But as they kept playing it over and over—"

"Oh, God…"

"—we decided we were proud of you."

"Really?"

"You father and I have worked with Ms. Fuller on several occasions. She is a wonderful teacher, who didn't deserve to be treated the way she was. So, even if it might give your father a hard time in the Senate hearings, we support your protest completely."

"Really?"

"Really." Mrs. Q finally acknowledged Billy in the backseat. "What did you think of it, Billy?"

Billy's mind must have been elsewhere. "What?"

"What did you think of Suzy's speech? Did you hear it?"

"I thought … I think … we might have a revolution on our hands."

Seven

MEMORIES AND OLD FRIENDS

"I CAN'T DO THIS anymore."

Billy was talking to himself. He'd spent the afternoon prepping Suzy's wand. It took a while to get the wires placed to perfectly match her intron's electromagnetic signature. By the time he was finished it was 7:30 in the evening, a perfect time to run over to Suzy's to have her try out her new magical powers.

That's when he started talking to himself. At least, he thought he was talking to himself.

"Can't do what, Billy?" his mom asked. She must have opened his door while he was so deep into building the wand that he hadn't noticed.

Billy nearly jumped out of his skin. Then he nearly jumped for joy. He thought Fame might have come back. When he realized it was his mother, he was disappointed. "Nothing, Mom."

"Wasn't it you who told me that nothing can ever be nothing."

Rats. Foiled by his own quantum quote. Billy had no choice but to answer his mom. "It's just that … I was okay with most of the world thinking I'm crazy, but now the Quinofskis think I am, too, and I hate that."

"Billy, believe it or not, I know exactly how you feel."

Billy believed it one hundred percent. He kicked himself for not asking her about this sooner. His mom might not know much, but she would certainly know all about his current situation.

She sat down on the bed next to him. "You know what I do when people think I'm crazy?"

"No, what?"

"The craziest thing I can think of. After that, for some reason, they think I'm okay."

"HANK, YOU SHOULD come see this."

Billy stood defiant in the Quinofskis' front lawn. With two hands over his head he held Suzy's wand like some guy he'd seen in a movie with a giant stereo. He was ready to stand there all night, but figured someone would call the General to let him know Billy was on his lawn.

After only a few minutes, he saw the curtains move before Mrs. Q called for her husband. Shortly after that, the curtain moved back further, and he locked eyes with the General.

"I'm not crazy," Billy shouted, knowing full well how crazy that made him sound. "And I'm not a bad influence on Suzy. If you'll give me five minutes, I think I can prove it."

The curtain closed. Billy didn't move. A moment later, the front door opened and out stepped General

Quinofski. With his hands in his pockets and his eyes gazing down, the great leader was humbled. "Come on in, Billy."

Billy walked past the General into the living room. Mrs. Q and Suzy were there. "Have a seat," said Suzy's mom.

Billy did. This wasn't the first time he'd seen their formal living room, but Billy thought it might have been the first time he'd sat on any of the furniture. He figured there was some name for the old-fashioned style the room was done up in, but he didn't know what it was, nor did he care.

General Quinofski didn't sit. "Billy, I owe you an apology. You've always been like a member of our family, and … well, I suppose this isn't the first time in history that one family member has misjudged another. I'm sorry for that."

"Uh, sir," said Billy. He stammered a bit. His long speech had just been pre-empted by the General's apology. After a few seconds, he found his mental footing again. "Thank you, but I don't blame you for thinking I'm unstable. I think that about myself sometimes. Maybe everyone does, I don't know. I bet a large part of you still thinks I might be."

"No, Billy." That was Mrs. Quinofski.

"It's okay, Mrs. Q," said Billy. "In a few minutes, you'll be questioning your sanity as much as mine."

The adults gave each other the kids-are-so-cute look, which made Suzy jump in. "Seriously, he's not kidding."

"General," said Billy, "do you have a video camera?"

"I think I have one around here somewhere." He asked his wife. "Honey?"

"Probably in the hall closet."

Billy asked the General, "Could you get it for me?"

When her father left to find the camera, Suzy asked Billy, "Do you think it's still on there?"

"I don't know," said Billy. "Whatever happened to our memories and the school reports wasn't perfect. It didn't get rid of the extra wands Peter made, or your glass tubes, stuff like that."

"What if it's not there?"

"Then we go with plan B."

"What's that?"

"No idea."

IT TOOK HALF AN HOUR to find the camera. The adults couldn't figure out why it wasn't where they thought it was supposed to be. The kids knew. Eventually, they found it in a box full of blank papers and empty note-books.

It was an old camera by Billy and Suzy's standards. It still used tape, and there was one inside.

"Play it," said Billy.

The four scrunched in together so they could all see the tiny screen. The General rewound the tape a bit, then hit play.

The scene was of the Quinofskis' basement, which had been emptied of most of the furniture. The General walked through the frame carrying three pairs of safety goggles. Billy stepped into the frame, taking his goggles from Suzy's father, who stepped out of frame. Billy, the one on the video, put the goggles on. In one hand he held a wooden magic wand.

"One big brunch buffet coming up," he said before he pushed the button on his wand.

Wham! Everything included in a four-star hotel breakfast buffet exploded from Billy's wand, knocking the camera over.

Back in the present, Billy and Suzy watched her dad see himself covered in food, laying on the floor.

"Oh, man!" On camera Billy rushed over to help the General to his feet. "I'm sorry, sir."

"That's okay, Billy, I'm fine."

In the present, the General's face was shock personified.

On camera Billy asked, "Suzy?"

She laid flat on her back in a sea of orange juice, scrambled eggs, hash browns, and ketchup. "I'm getting used to it." She looked down at her feet. "The cat's a new addition, though."

Sure enough, Fame, in her black feline form, licked pancake syrup off Suzy's toes.

"Oh, that's Fame," said Billy, "my, uh…"

Suzy asked, "Cat?"

"No," said Billy, "I mean, yes."

"You don't have a cat," said Suzy.

Back in the living room she said, "You still don't."

Billy ignored Suzy's joke. Instead, he asked her father, "Is it coming back to you?"

The General stopped the camera and reached for a chair. "I need to sit down."

Mrs. Q had yet to have a revelation. It was as if she hadn't seen the video. "I don't understand. What are you all talking about? Hank, when did you make that movie?"

"Operation Hocus Pocus," said the General.

"Oh, great," said Suzy. "Of all the things that could have stayed forgotten, Dad remembers that stupid name!"

"I'M NOT SURE I've recalled everything."

It took about an hour for his memories to come together. The General remembered setting up Operation Hocus Pocus, but they never successfully made wands for his soldiers. He remembered Billy hexing kids who tried to beat him up, and how that led to Billy's plan to save the captured soldiers in Kashmir by following their families' thoughts.

Mrs. Quinofski still waited for her "a-ha" moment. "I'm not sure you all have your heads screwed on straight."

"There's one thing I don't understand," said the General. "How did we lose our memories?"

"We're not sure," said Billy. "All we know is we have to get my wand back from the Quantum World. I'm hoping we can use this wand I made for Suzy to do that."

"What do you have in mind, soldier?" General Quinofski used to call Billy that when he was very young. This time it came out with more respect.

Billy had given this a good bit of thought, but he hadn't had a chance to voice his ideas with anyone until now. He began to walk around the room in circles while running his fingers through his thick blonde hair and muttering, "Where to start? Where to start?"

"What's he doing?" asked Mrs. Quinofski.

Suzy read Billy's body language like a favorite old book. "Thinking."

"I believe the reason we haven't seen the Teacher or…" Billy stopped himself. Fame was still a secret to everyone but Suzy. He'd nearly slipped up and mentioned her in front of everyone.

"Who?" asked Mrs. Quinofski.

Suzy didn't want Billy's stream of consciousness dammed up so she answered. "He's a quantum being, Mom. He was Merlin and about every other long, gray-haired old man in history."

"Merlin wasn't history, honey," said her mom. "He's a literary figure."

"Actually," said Billy. He stopped walking in circles like he was going to say something, then didn't and started pacing again. "Never mind. Whether he's historical or literary, he's a being of the collective unconsciousness. Nearly everyone has an image of a wise old man or wizard. That image creates thoughts, and thoughts are real. They give him power."

"And he's really smart," said Suzy.

The General got the conversation back on track. "You were saying?"

Billy picked up where he left off. "I think the reason we haven't seen him is because we haven't done any magic." He held out the wand to Suzy. "Are you up for it?"

"Is it safe?" asked Suzy's Mom.

"That depends, Mrs. Q."

"On what?"

"On if she gets scared."

"I'm already scared," said Suzy, "so we can mark that as a 'no' for safe."

THERE WAS SOME DISCUSSION about what kind of magic Suzy should do. Billy knew that simple stuff could be done without entering the Quantum World, which would be a safe way to start. General Quinofski said he was getting tired of his wife saying they were all crazy. He suggested moving the furniture out of the basement like they did for Billy's breakfast buffet, only with magic. They set up the camera like they had before. Everyone put on safety goggles.

"Picture the furniture out on the lawn," said Billy. "Think of a word that locks the image in your head and tap the button."

"A magic word?"

Billy picked up on Suzy's sarcastic tone. "Yes, get over it. A magic word, okay?"

"Okay, a magic word. Not a problem."

"Remember to just tap the button."

"Tap it?" asked Suzy.

"Yeah. It'll take a little pressure, but don't leave your finger on it, or you'll be in the Quantum World with no idea what part of the universe your hand has gotten off to."

Suzy took a wide stance facing the living room area of her basement biology lab. "Okay, here we go." She raised her new wand. "Move furniture," she said, and tapped the button.

Wham! A bright white light flashed from the wand, and a loud crack of thunder shook the basement, as all of the furniture in the room popped out of existence.

The shaking thunder came from the air rushing into the space that the furniture once occupied.

"That was awesome!" said Suzy. "Mom, did you see that!?"

But Suzy's mom was nowhere to be seen.

"Mom!" screamed Suzy. "Mom!"

"Janice?!" the General called out.

Billy thought he heard something so he shushed them. Sure enough, from outside they heard a woman in hysterics. They all ran out to find Mrs. Quinofski laughing, gasping, and twirling around like a kid who just finished her first rollercoaster ride. "Wow!" she said, before collapsing with laughter on the couch in their front lawn. "That scared the stuffing out of me!"

"Mom, are you all right?"

"I don't know. Am I?"

Suzy asked Billy, "What happened?"

"My guess would be that since your mom was outside with the furniture the first time, and you pictured making it the same as it was then, she popped out as well."

Mrs. Quinofski moved her jaw around to try and clear her ears. "Popped is right."

"Honey, are you okay?"

Billy was always amazed at the different tones of voice the General had. Asking about his wife's well-being made him sound like a lost little boy.

"I'm fine, Hank," she said, "and what's more, I'm remembering."

The General noticed the passing traffic of the base. "This probably isn't the best place to have total recall. Suzy, could you put the furniture back?"

"I don't know," said Suzy. She turned to Billy. "Can I?"

"My favorite do-over magic word," he said. "Oops."

Suzy giggled. "Okay. One do-over coming up." She held up the wand, said "Oops" and tapped the button.

Furniture and people disappeared from the lawn with a clap of thunder and landed back in the basement as if they'd never left. Except for one thing, there was one more person than there was before.

"YOU'RE BACK!"

Billy ran up to the old man sitting on the couch like he expected him to get up and give him a hug, but the man just sat there, so Billy had to stop short.

"Actually, I never really left," he said.

"Excuse me," said Mrs. Quinofski, "who are you and how did you get into my house?"

"I'm sorry, Janice," he said with perfect manners, "May I call you Janice?"

"Uh…"

He didn't wait for her to figure out her preference. "I don't believe we met the last time you saw me, but if you recall, it was after Billy brought the soldiers back from captivity."

Mrs. Quinofski's face flushed as the memory filled her head. "Yes. You showed up to explain how those men died."

"Mrs. Q," said Billy, by way of introduction, "This is … okay, this is hard because quantum beings don't have names, but I call him The Teacher."

Billy thought Mrs. Quinofski was still occupied with returning memories, but she responded out of reflex. "Nice to meet you."

Billy got back to the matters at hand with the Teacher. "Where have you been?"

"You wished me away."

"I wished the wand away," said Billy. "Not you."

"I suppose in your subconscious we're a package deal. It took Suzy's use of the wand to make you believe we could talk again."

"But you were in our dreams," said Suzy.

"Dreams are where your world meets mine," said the Teacher. "Though the language of human subconscious is hard to manage."

"They have my wand," said Billy. *They* is what the Teacher called the evil forces in the Quantum World.

"They do and they don't."

"What does that mean?" asked General Quinofski.

The Teacher thought for a moment, which always gave Billy the feeling he was mentally traveling back to the beginning of Time and forward to its end. Finally, the old man said, "Are you familiar with the Taoist symbol for Yin and Yang?"

"Of course," said General Quinofski.

"Ah," said Billy, "can you refresh my memory?"

The Teacher explained, "It's a circle bisected by an S. One side is white, with a little bit of black at its center. The other is black, with a little dot of white. Of all the philosophical symbols in human history, this one best describes the nature of existence. Light and Shadow, Right and Wrong, Good and Evil. They are not only co-dependent, but sometimes are one and the same."

"What does that mean for my wand?" asked Billy.

"We," said the Teacher, "on one side of the circle are

trying to prevent the wand from being used by the other side. We are not always successful. In fact, *We* are not immune to the motivations of the other side."

General Quinofski could appreciate the importance of this philosophy lesson, but he was also a man of action. "Practically speaking, sir, what are you talking about?"

"As long as *We* can protect the wand from *Them* — and our own selfish pursuits — then it has less effect. Right now, small ripples of the dark half have been radiating from our world to yours."

"What does that mean?" asked Suzy.

"It means that troubled times are ahead. They have always encouraged ignorance and paranoia. They are the enemies of empathy. They feed off the dark side of human imagination. By turning human against human, they reap the benefit of the ingenuity with which your kind hate and kill each other. Billy's wand, though it is protected, still has amplified their influence in your world. Maybe you've noticed."

"They're the ones behind the new school rules and horrible textbooks," said Suzy.

"No doubt," said the Teacher. "Young minds are easier to control. They love to wield influence in schools and youth programs."

Billy put two and two together. "Like the Hitler Youth?" Like every other geeky boy his age, Billy rarely missed a World War II documentary on the History channel.

"Exactly," said the Teacher.

General Quinofski eyed a file on his desk about the

history of Saudi Arabia and how the schools came into play there. "I can think of a few others." He didn't elaborate but got a nod of affirmation from the Teacher.

"And all those crazy terrorists Dad has to deal with," said Suzy.

"Evil has always had a good foothold among zealots, Suzy, but yes, Billy's wand has made them stronger."

The General added. "I can think of a few senators who have become emboldened lately."

"Politicians are an easy target for both sides."

Billy cocked his head. "Both sides?"

The Teacher stroked his beard and got a little twinkle in his eye. "Evil can influence a weak mind, Billy, and Goodness can inspire a strong one. Greatness will rise to the occasion. That's one of the best aspects of your species. You excel in times of challenge."

"Does Evil ever win?" asked Mrs. Quinofski.

"Yes, it does," said the Teacher. "Not forever, but for always."

"That doesn't make any sense," said Suzy.

"At any given time somewhere on the planet among the human race, Evil has won a major victory. Tyrants, despots, genocides, some corporations, some laws, some court decisions, all have been victories for the dark half of that Zen circle. They happen in every generation. The fight of Good vs. Evil is never ending." He held the kids' hands. "Thanks to your wands, Billy and Suzy, you are now in the thick of the battle."

"What happens if…?" Billy was too afraid to say the worst out loud.

The Teacher said it for him. "If *They* obtain the full

power of your wand? They'll punch a hole between our world and yours. They will manifest themselves here and that will be horrible."

"Has that happened before?" asked Suzy.

"The Dark Ages. The Spanish Inquisition. The World Wars. Bad times for both our kinds, some lasting hundreds of years, when superstition, fear, and the occult ruled over reason."

"What can we do about it?" asked Billy.

The Teacher sighed and stroked his beard a couple of times. "It's not going to be easy. Getting your wand back will be a good start."

"How do we do that?" asked Suzy.

The Teacher sat in silence.

"He can't tell us," said Billy.

Suzy was confused. "Why not?"

"Because he's one of *Them*."

"What?"

"I don't understand it completely," said Billy. "All I know is that he's told me that if he knows what we're going to do, then *They* do. I think that's what Evil was trying to tell me in my dreams."

"Billy's right," said the Teacher. "I am one of them. I have that little opposite dot within my soul."

No one said anything. The Teacher stood. "So, I will take my leave." He instructed the kids. "Billy, Suzy, get the wand, and your teacher, back." To General Quinofski he said, "Sir, beware those with good intentions."

"They are a pain my backside right now," he said. "I'll try to keep them at bay."

"Janice," the Teacher said to Mrs. Quinofski, "you

have such an abundance of goodness. Share it with them. They will need it."

With that, the Teacher disappeared in a slow fade.

"SO WHAT'S THE PLAN?"

General Quinofski got right to work after their mysterious house guest left, but he was quickly interrupted.

"Meow."

The innocent call of a cat outside the basement door made Billy and Suzy grin from ear to ear. Suzy opened the door. "Fame!"

The black cat trotted inside and jumped into Billy's arms. "That's my cat," he told the adults. "I thought I'd lost her."

You did, thought Fame inside the heads of Billy and Suzy.

"Do you think she's hungry?" asked Mrs. Quinofski.

Please, not cat food!

"She's a finicky eater," said Billy. "Maybe some water."

Got anything stronger? I am, like, over a thousand years old.

Billy and Suzy both stifled a giggle. While Mrs. Quinofski went to get some water, her husband eyed the cat with suspicion. Billy ran interference. "You were saying, sir?"

Billy's question brought him back to the issues at hand. "You know more about the Quantum World than anyone else, Billy, so I was wondering if you have a plan."

"Not really, sir." He threw a thought toward Fame. *Do you know where my wand is?*

It's in the Quantum World, she thought back at him. *That means it's everywhere and nowhere all at once.*

Suzy noticed a marked change in Billy's behavior. "Uh-oh."

"What?" asked her father.

"Billy's thinking again."

Billy began to pace.

No one said anything until Mrs. Quinofski showed up with a bowl. "Here's some water." She put the bowl down next to Fame who didn't take her eyes off Billy. "That's a very attentive cat."

No one said anything while Billy paced. The silence became uncomfortable. "He could be like this for days," said Suzy.

"Suzy," said her father, "why don't you walk him home?"

"Sure." She took Billy by the shoulders and guided him toward the door. Fame followed.

Before they left, the General said, "Billy, I'm sorry I ever doubted you."

Billy broke his stupor to crack a sad smile. "Glad to have you back, sir."

"ANYTHING I CAN DO?"

Suzy had experience with Billy's brainstorms. She knew when to check on him and when to stay quiet and out of the way. She walked beside him in silence until they were past the guard gate and out of earshot from soldiers and civilians.

"I don't know," he said. "I don't know. I don't know. I don't know. Fame?"

He asked the cat, but his answer came from a human tomboy in jeans, a T-shirt, baseball cap, and sleeveless jean jacket. "Getting the wand's not going to be a problem. You think of it, and it'll show up. Keeping it is another issue."

"Why can't I use my wand to make it appear here and now?" asked Suzy.

"If it were some random object from an alternate timeline," said Billy, "you probably could. But I'm betting it would be hard to sneak the wand out of the Quantum World.

Fame confirmed Billy's hypothesis. "It would be your thoughts against everyone in the Quantum World. You wouldn't stand a chance."

"Would it be better if we were on your home turf?" asked Billy.

"A better chance of getting the wand, yes. But keeping it, and pulling it through to your side? I don't see how that'll be possible."

"Good," said Billy.

"How is that good?" asked Suzy.

"Because if Fame can see how, *They* can see how and defend against it."

"Okay, then back to my question," said Suzy. "What can I do?"

"Practice clearing your mind," said Billy, "because, however we do this, we're going into the Quantum World, where your thoughts and emotions become reality. If you don't stay focused, trust me, it gets bad."

Eight

THE BATTLE IS MET

"CRAP!" After not being able to sleep all night, Billy suddenly found that he'd overslept and would be late for school. Not that there was school to go to. He watched the coverage of the protest on the *Today* show as he got dressed.

"Kids In Power! Kids In Power!" was the chant that echoed from the halls into the national news media. Billy wasn't sure, but he had a feeling that the cryptic K.I.P. on their hall pass might have stood for something else. The broadcast also played Suzy's speech over and over.

"You've got them on their heels now, son," said Billy's mother. "All they need is one good push."

Billy smiled to himself. A few days ago he would have

dismissed her comment as paranoid babbling. Now he understood exactly what she was talking about. "I don't know about that, Mom. They are pretty powerful."

Together they watched as a reporter spoke live from Suzy's front doorstep. "As you said, Matt, the girl who gave that impassioned speech is the daughter of General Quinofski, who has been on the Senate hot seat for weeks."

Billy ignored the backstory. *Fame*, he thought. *Is Suzy watching this?*

Yep, came Fame's voice only in his head. *She says hi.*
Tell her I guess I won't be walking with her to school today.
She says to keep watching.

Moments later, Suzy came out of the front door, escorted by her parents. In seconds she was surrounded by microphones.

"I said pretty much what I wanted to say yesterday."

Billy had a hard time realizing that it had been less than twenty-four hours since the protest started at school. So much had happened in such a short time.

A reporter asked Suzy about her dad. "Our issues at school and Dad's issues at work have nothing to do with each other."

Fame, thought Billy, *remind Suzy what the Teacher told us about how They use fear and stuff.*

Billy watched on TV as another reporter tried to ask a question, but Suzy wasn't listening. "Wait," she said. "It's not quite true that these things aren't related. We are in a constant battle against paranoia, fear, and ignorance. As my biology teacher taught me, knowledge is like freedom. It must be constantly fought for and protected. All of the soldiers on this base, all of the soldiers in America, have sworn an oath to defend the Constitution. They will fight, and if necessary die, to protect words on a page. Our teachers fight every day to teach us about words like those. And yes, we have enemies. Believe me, my dad's a general, I know all about our enemies. They have been raised on the same paranoia and fear that we have to fight every day. Some of them are ignorant of the beautiful words of their own religion, because they have only been taught the ugly ones.

"The people who fired Ms. Fuller are just as afraid, just as paranoid, and just as ignorant as our enemies. In my mind, they are the enemy among us."

With the reporters silenced by Suzy's speech, she and her parents got in the car to go to school.

BILLY CAUGHT A RIDE from Peter, who raced him to school so fast that they saw Suzy arrive to cheering fans. Billy pushed his way through the crowd to get to her.

She grabbed his arm and pulled him into private conversation range. "Holy crap! I'm popular!"

"Fame is fleeting," said Billy.

"Like a cat," she said with a wink.

Linda and Charles came out of the school to meet Suzy. "You were great this morning," said Linda.

Suzy barely heard her, not so much because of the noise, but because she was waiting for Charles to say something. Still, she managed to say "Thanks."

Billy noticed Linda's hair was haggard and she was wearing the same thing she had worn yesterday. "Did you two spend the night at school?"

"We did," said Linda. "We have broken up into three shifts to keep the sit-in going."

"But that's not important right now," said Charles. "Suzy, the Federal School Board has called a meeting with Dillon, the local school board, and us. We want you to join us."

"Really?" said Suzy. Her attention got lost in Charles's eyes until Billy nudged her elbow. "Can Billy come, too?"

"Sure," said Charles. "You've both been voted into the protest committee."

SHOOT ME. PLEASE, shoot me now.

Billy was glad to have Fame back, especially during a meeting as boring as this one. He was able to pass mental messages back and forth to Suzy through Fame, even though Fame was nowhere to be seen.

The meeting was less a conference of equals and more a lecture from the Federal Board to everyone else at the table. The students could only take solace in the fact that they weren't the only ones being treated like children. Billy had the unfortunate luck to be seated next to Principal Dillon, so he had to pretend to pay attention, instead of surreptitiously reading something fun under the table, like a college physics book he'd recently downloaded to his Kindle app.

All the while, the first shift of protestors kept chanting, "Kids In Power! Kids In Power!" through the school halls.

Billy's eyes were about to roll into the back of his head, when he noticed that some of the adults were passing notes. This amazed him for two reasons: First, had they not heard of text messaging? Second, they're teachers! Shouldn't they know better? Billy had seen some of the ones passing notes write up students for doing the same thing in their classes. Oh, the shame of it all!

The chanting crept back into his boredom. He put the two observations together, and jotted down, "K.I.P.?" on a piece of scrape paper and showed it Dillon.

Dillon wrote back, "Knowledge Is Power."

Wanna hear something funny? He thought to Fame.

Sure, she thought back.

Well, yeah, you too, but pass it on to Suzy.

Of course.

Tell her, the K.I.P. thing on the Hall Pass… It doesn't stand for Kids In Power. Dillon told me it means Knowledge Is Power.

She said, 'That's not funny, that's brilliant.'

"Really?" Everyone stopped talking and looked at Billy. "Sorry. Was that out loud?" They all smirked and went back to their lecturing and ignoring.

Fame passed on another thought: *Now that was funny.*

Is that what Suzy said?

No, thought Fame, *I did. Suzy can't stop laughing.*

Great.

She did say, 'Pass a note to Dillon. Ask if his K.I.P. could meet with our K.I.P. -- meaning the students.

Billy did as she asked. Dillon wrote back, "Absolutely. At lunch."

"Where?" wrote Billy.

Dillon had some fun with the answer. "Duh! Stoner's Row, dude."

✳

"I NEED A CIGARETTE."

Hanging out with Principal Dillon, a handful of teachers, some adults Billy didn't know, and a bunch of seniors behind the gym during lunch was totally weird. Even more weird since they all had to sneak around to meet up without raising suspicions.

"Really, Mrs. Marshall?" said Linda. "After all of those times you wrote me up for smoking?"

"Yes," said Mrs. Marshall, a teacher that Billy and Suzy had seen around but never had a class with. "I'm sorry about that. Have you got one?"

"No," said Linda. "You talked me into quitting."

"Great." Her tone was sarcastic. "After this is all done, you're going to have to tell me how you made it stick."

"We don't have much time," said Dillon. "Billy, why did you want to meet?"

"Don't look at me, sir. It was Suzy's idea."

"K.I.P.," said Suzy. "I take it that's a code to identify sympathizers?"

"Yes," said Dillon. "Knowledge Is Power."

Linda was confused, "Not Kids In Power?"

"It can be both," said Suzy to avoid losing the subject. "Here's my idea." She shifted her weight a little bit like she was going to physically throw her idea at them. "Join us."

The adults rolled their eyes and sighed. "Don't you think we want to?" asked Dillon.

"It's not so simple," said Mrs. Maltin, the librarian. "We have to protect our jobs. We have more to lose than students."

"Really?" asked Billy. "I heard teachers are paid so little that almost any job would pay better, and we have our whole futures on the line."

"For those of you who haven't met Billy and Suzy," said Dillon, "you will find them to be admirable debaters."

"If we all stick together," said Suzy, "no one will lose their jobs."

Linda spoke up. "If we don't hang together, by Heavens we'll all hang separately." She smiled. "Ms. Fuller taught me that, and until now I didn't really understand it."

"But we can't walk in there and say we think it's okay to take over the school," said a teacher that neither Billy nor Suzy knew.

"Why not?" asked Suzy. "They did it. We're trying to take it back."

Dillon stepped up to the plate. "Anton? How would the teachers' union feel about that?"

"We're in 100 percent agreement with the students," said the guy who must have been Anton. "We want Ms. Fuller back to work, the cameras out of the classroom, and the textbooks thrown out."

"I have to say," said the unknown teacher, "I liked the idea of the cameras for security when they first came in."

"What if…" Suzy lost her balance a bit at the sound of Charles's voice. He repeated himself once he had everyone's attention. "What if the footage from the cameras were somehow locked away and could only be accessed by a warrant?"

"You're pre-law, right?" asked Mrs. Marshall, the smoker.

"I'm still in high school, Mrs. Marshall," Charles said.

"Sorry. I lose track of you kids sometimes."

Dillon might have gained some sense of command but not technical knowledge. "I have no idea what happens to the footage."

Anton did. "The footage goes straight to the intranet."

"Not a problem," said Billy. "That's easily password protected with an encryption key."

"The Chief of Police could have the key, not to be used without a court order," said Charles.

"Could we have two keys?" Anton asked. "One with either the police or the superintendent and one with the union?"

Dillon asked his computer expert. "Billy?"

"Sure. I could program that in my sleep, so I know it can be done."

"We all want Ms. Fuller back," said Dillon, "so that's not an issue."

"The old textbooks are in the library's offsite storage," said Mrs. Maltin. "We could have them back in a day or two."

Dillon made silent eye contact with each of the adults. They all gave an almost imperceptible nod. Dillon then summed up. "Kids, it looks like we have a Scooby Doo ending."

Billy, Suzy, Charles, and Linda all had question marks on their faces. "We don't know what that means," said Linda.

"It means, that thanks to you meddlesome kids, this might turn out okay."

"WE, ALL OF US LOCALLY, want to say, we're joining the sit-in."

The afternoon session was very different than the one in the morning. When Dillon, the local school board, and the teachers' union all sided with the students, the federal negotiator got defensive. There was a lot of screaming, shouting, and text messaging for advice. Billy stopped listening almost immediately. He had to come up with a plan to get his wand back.

One thing kept echoing in his mind, *Knowledge Is Power*. General Quinofski said that Billy knew the Quantum World better than anyone. So how could he turn his knowledge into power? What did he know about Quantum Mechanics that would allow him to possess something without the Quantum Biologics knowing he had it?

Since Fame and the Teacher can read his thoughts, how can he have the wand and not think about having it? How can he know something and not know it at the same time?

Billy popped up in his seat. "Oh, it's so simple!"

Once again, every eye in the room landed on Billy. "I'm sorry. Was that out loud again?"

Nine

ABSOLUTELY UNCERTAIN

I T WAS FRIDAY AFTERNOON, and Billy was going to need his brother's help, so he lay in wait for Peter's brief moment at home between work and going out with his friends. Sometimes Billy got the feeling the only reason Peter bothered coming home at all was to yell at him about their mother, but that wasn't his thought at the moment. Billy would only have the briefest of seconds to jog Peter's memory, and he didn't have nearly as much to work with as he did with the Quinofskis.

As soon as Peter walked in the front door, Billy pounced. "Do you remember making these?" He showed him the remaining split wands that he'd taken from Peter's shop.

"No," Peter said flatly, barely glancing at them on his way to his room. While he worked the lock on his bedroom door, he asked. "What are they?"

"Magic wands," said Billy.

"Don't be stupid. I would never do anything that lame." With that, Billy's window of opportunity closed. Peter retreated into his room. Billy was crestfallen. If the wands didn't work, he didn't know what he would do.

Then Peter crept back into the living room. "Did I take you two geeks to the mall?"

"Yes!" Billy said more to himself than to answer Peter's question.

"We bought a whole bunch of magic wands and I split them down the middle for you."

"Yeah," said Billy. "You did a great job."

"Dude, you blew up the school!"

"Well, not the whole school."

"Awesome."

"I told you!" said their mother, who was walking in from her bedroom. "I knew you two had been getting along."

They both ignored her. "Why did I forget about that?" asked Peter.

"I don't know," said Billy, "but you're not the only one. We're working on that, but right now…" Billy handed Peter a big block of cedar wood. "I need a favor."

"HEY, BRAINS-FOR-BRAINS, your box is done."

Billy opened the door to find his brother in full yawn, leaning against the jamb, and looking like he'd worked through the night. Billy, on the other hand, went to bed early so he popped out of his room spry and fully aware that he might face anything and everything before the day was over.

The project appeared to be a simple block of wood about a foot-and-a-half long and six inches high and deep. It was beautifully polished, and had Billy not known better, he would have thought it was a single piece. He took the block from Peter. "Wow, this is perfect."

"It better be, I spent all night on it."

"Thanks, Peter."

"Are you sure you don't want to know how it works?" asked Peter.

"Positive," said Billy.

"All right, but you'll never get it open by guessing, I promise you."

"Good." Billy studied the box more closely. "So you didn't go out last night?"

"How could I? You said you needed that right away."

"Yeah, but you could have said no."

Peter held Billy's eye contact. "No I couldn't." He then studied a spot on the wall. "Besides, my date cancelled. Said she was busy."

"You mean Linda?" Billy held his tone as steady as he could.

Peter didn't answer right away, but when he did it was straight up to Billy's face. Not harsh, but honest and fast. "Yeah."

Billy nodded. "I thought so."

"Linda seemed to think you'd have a problem with that."

"Me?" asked Billy. "Why should I have a problem with that? I don't have a problem with that. I mean, it's not like I have any reason to have a problem, right?"

"How old are you again?"

"Thirteen, why?"

Peter half-smiled. "It gets better, little brain. I promise you, it gets better."

"YOU READY FOR THIS?"

Billy showed up at Suzy's house later that morning with his new block of wood. "What's with that?" asked Suzy.

Billy walked past her into the house. "The less you know about it, the better."

"What's that supposed to mean?" Suzy followed.

"Don't take it personally. I don't even know everything about it. They can read our thoughts, remember?"

"Oh, yeah."

Billy ran into the General and Mrs. Quinofski in the kitchen. "Good morning, Billy," said Mrs. Q. "Would you like some breakfast?"

"No, thanks," said Billy. "I'd like my wand back."

"SURE, IT COULD BE SCARY, but so can a bad dream or a good movie."

It took a bit of convincing from both Billy and Suzy before her parents would consent to what they thought was a dangerous mission. What finally won the day was the job Billy had for them.

"We need you to stay here and think good thoughts about us," said Billy. "You will be our anchor."

"I can do that," said Mrs. Q.

Suzy thought she might be able to do that a bit too well, since somehow everything Suzy did in school always got reported back her mom. She wondered if her mom knew that everyone in town called her "The Boss."

"Suzy!" said Billy. Apparently, he had been saying something to her.

"Sorry, my mind wandered off."

"What did I tell you about that?" asked Billy. "Your mind can't wander off where we're going. You have to focus."

"Okay," said Suzy. She wasn't used to Billy telling her what to do, and she didn't want him to get used to doing it.

"You have to grab on tight," said Billy.

"I understand." Her patience was clearly running thin.

Billy picked up the signals. "Sorry. It's just ..." he didn't want to admit he was afraid.

"I've been there before, Billy, remember?"

Billy gave a small nod. "How could I forget?"

Everyone laughed more than the joke about their memory deserved and some tension released. General Quinofski finally set up the video camera. He and Mrs. Q put on goggles. Billy said he and Suzy wouldn't need them. The kids stood in the middle of the room. In one hand Suzy held her wand, Billy his block of wood. With the other, they held each other's hands.

Suzy was surprised by how firm Billy's grip was. She flexed her fingers and smiled at him.

"What?" asked Billy.

"Nothing," said Suzy.

"Do you remember what to do?"

She decided not to chastise Billy for asking him to re-peat the simplest instructions she'd had since kinder-garten. Instead, she answered with a flat tone. "Count to five, concentrate on you, find Mom and Dad's thoughts, follow them home, and let go of the button."

"And hold on tight," said Billy. "Let's do it."

"Think good thoughts," Suzy told her parents. She held up the wand and pressed the button.

"HOLY—!"

Suzy didn't get to finish her exclamation, as she was whipped around in the darkness. She could feel Billy's hand. She could feel the sensation of free fall. She could feel tornado-like wind on her face. Then suddenly she slammed into Billy and her body weighed three times what it normally did. She felt like—

"We're on a roller coaster!" shouted Billy.

"How did we get here?"

"I have no idea. We're following your thoughts. What's the last thing you remember?"

"You said, 'hold on tight.' I guess that made me think of a— HEYYYYYY!"

This was without a doubt, the biggest, scariest rollercoaster in the universe.

Billy eventually caught his breath enough to say, "Think of something else!"

And just that quickly, they were floating among white billowing clouds. Rainbows spilled from one to the next and pink unicorns in tutus and ballet slippers pranced all around. "Did you ever hear the song—?" started Suzy.

Billy stopped her. "Don't sing it, or we'll never get out of here." Billy knew the YouTube viral song she was thinking of and did everything he could not to think of it, too. It didn't work. "Just count to five," he told her.

"One."

The clouds turned to mud, the rainbows into rain. The unicorns were replaced by evil yard gnomes all chattering things Billy couldn't make out. Suzy could, though. They were numbers. Every number in the universe, every equation ever conceived by man or nature forced their way into Suzy's head. She nearly exploded.

"Billy! What comes after one?"

"They're trying to keep us here! Forget the counting, find your parent's thoughts. They'll look like strands of color. They'll come out of nowhere and wrap around us."

Before she could search for them, she noticed the number chanting in her head had stopped. The rain had stopped. For a brief second, there was no sound at all.

Then the gnomes lined up to sing that stupid song, and rainbows appeared from everywhere. "I can't find the thoughts," said Suzy. "There are too many rainbows."

A flash of blood-red lightning filled the sky, and a low roll of thunder sent a cold chill into their bones. In the distance, Billy saw black streaks of smoke heading their way. He knew from his last trip inside the Quantum World what that was.

Death.

What could he do? He didn't have his wand. Suzy's thoughts were infected by the gnomes. If he couldn't get them away from her, she'd never be able to release the button.

As sparks of energy popped around his head, Billy realized that, inside the Quantum World, he didn't need his wand. It was what brought him there, but once inside, everything was up to imagination.

And he'd dealt with gnomes before!

"Banish gnomes!" he shouted, and with a sweep of his arm blew them away as if they were tissue paper in the coming storm.

The streaks of death still arched toward them. Billy grabbed Suzy and said, "*Scutum absconditum.*" His invisible force field still held up around his mobile home. He hoped it was strong enough to keep out the approaching doom.

Apparently, it worked. Billy and Suzy huddled inside a glass-like ball that the smoke couldn't penetrate. Billy relaxed a little, but could feel Suzy shaking in his arms.

"It's okay," he told her. "We're safe for now."

Suzy looked around at the curling smoke that engulfed them outside the shield. It twisted and churned as if it had a mind of its own and were trying to find a way in. "What is that stuff?"

"I've seen it before," said Billy. "It's death."

"And you came up with 'Invisible Force Field' to stop it?"

"Yeah, so?"

"Kind of geeky, don't you think?"

"Hey, I said it in Latin."

"Billy, *Tantum geeks Latine loqui.*" (NOTE: only geeks speak Latin).

"Yeah, well, Peter didn't think I was a geek for speaking Latin. He thought it was cool."

"Really?" She then realized, "I don't care. Let's get the wand and get out of here."

"We might already have it." Billy held up his block of wood. "It's both inside here, and it's not."

But Suzy wasn't listening. She looked over Billy's shoulder and screamed. The black smoke became the solid flesh and bone of a gigantic head of an angry, scary old man. "That's the Teacher!"

But the Teacher wasn't himself. His persona was dark, dangerous, and evil. He was also so large that Billy's little invisible force field was like a tiny pill to him. With a mighty roar, the giant teacher swallowed Billy and Suzy — force field and all.

"Scutum absconditum."
   "Scutum absconditum."
   "Scutum absconditum."

Cracks in the force field spidered across the sphere that protected Billy and Suzy, as teeth the size of two story houses gnashed down on them. It was all Billy could do to keep his mind off the Discovery Science shows he'd seen discussing bite pressures and on the invincibility of his imaginary force field. Between Latin chants, he managed an instruction to Suzy. "Find your parents' thoughts."

"How? I can't see them."

"Open your eyes!"

Sure enough, Suzy had covered her eyes when the Teacher engulfed them. "That would help, huh?" She opened them to see that they were inside a giant mouth that was trying to crack their outer shell like a walnut. "Oh, God!" said Suzy. "I was wrong, that did not help!" Still, she kept her eyes open, hopeful for any signs of streaming colors of thought.

Nothing.

"How am I supposed to see them from inside his mouth?" she asked.

"They're thoughts," said Billy. "*Scutum absconditum. Scutum absconditum.* They should be visible through anything."

"But they have no idea where we are."

"That shouldn't matter," said Billy, but she had given him an idea. "*Scutum absconditum.* Send your thoughts out to them."

"What?!"

"Think of your parents. Think of your lab. Use your love to find theirs."

Suzy closed her eyes to concentrate, and soon their little sphere filled with pink mist. "It can't get out of the shield."

"Of course it can," said Billy. "It's love, some stupid shield I made up can't stop it." As he said that, the giant Teacher bit down hard. The shield cracked badly. Spit, chewed-up food, and blood from his gums flooded their sanctuary.

At the same time, Suzy's pink mist flew out. "Grab onto it!" shouted Billy.

"But, it's vapor!"

"Just do it!"

Suzy grabbed onto the pink cloud but actually caught a silk scarf in her hand. She recognized it as the first birthday present she'd bought for her mom all by herself. It pulled her out of the sphere. Billy managed to grab her ankle with one hand to go along for the ride. In his other hand he clutched the block of wood and cursed himself for not asking Peter for a handle.

Outside the sphere, but still inside the giant evil Teacher, the scarf dove down the esophagus toward what Billy was sure to be a bath of stomach acid. "Why are we going down? We should let go!"

"No," said Suzy. "Not yet. We have to go down past the uvula to get from the oropharynx to the nasopharynx."

"Naso? Does that mean what I think it means?"

No sooner did he say that, then the scarf looped up a passage in the back of the enormous throat. "Yes," said Suzy. "We're going through the nasal passages."

"Let's hope he doesn't have allergies." Billy got a mouthful of snot, before he realized that shouting up at Suzy probably wasn't a good idea.

"No," she said, "let's hope he does."

"Why?" He wasn't sure she could hear him with his head down and them flying through snot-covered tissue like two kids inner-tubing in a mossy swamp.

"Because then he'll snee—"

Before she could finish her sentence, everything flew toward a light at the end of the giant tunnel. Billy, Suzy, the scarf of love, and everything two kids could imagine might be inside an old man's nostrils blew through the Teacher's nose hairs into who knew what.

In their freefall, Suzy saw strands of bright colors whipping around the Quantum World like the Aurora Borealis. The scarf took off after them with the kids and the wooden box in tow.

"When we stop," shouted Billy, "think that we have only been gone a nanosecond, and then take your finger off the button."

Suzy suppressed the urge to tease Billy about the

specifics of a nanosecond, versus a split-second, or just-a-second. Instead, she concentrated hard on her hand, specifically, her finger holding down the button on the wand.

So much so in fact, that she nearly didn't hear Billy say, "Now!"

"DID YOU GET IT?"

Suzy ignored her parents' concern over her and Billy's health, and whatever incredibly horrible smelling stuff they were covered in. She wanted to know if Billy got the wand.

Billy was more concerned with the yuck-factor. "Suzy, do everyone a favor, picture us in clean clothes, and tap the button."

"Us, too," said her father. That's when she realized she must have hugged them the instant they got back. "What is this stuff?"

"Snot mostly," said Billy. "Also some spit, probably Quantum bacteria, and a fair amount of blood."

"The Teacher should really floss," said Suzy. "Bleeding gums can lead to heart disease."

"Thank you, Dr. Quinofski," said Billy. "Now, could you do the cleanup thing, please?"

Suzy giggled a little bit, then repeated the instructions. "Picture us all in clean clothes, and tap the button."

"Yes," said Billy, "A light, quick tap."

Suzy giggled a little bit more and did as she was told.

Poof! The smell and yuck were gone. General Quinofski was in a crisp new uniform. Mrs. Q wore her favorite thing in the world, comfortable sweat pants and an old T-shirt.

"Wow," said Mrs. Quinofski to Billy, "you clean up nice."

Suzy's giggle became a full-on laugh.

"What did you do?" asked Billy. He checked himself in a mirror. Suzy had magically dressed him in sharp pair of black slacks, Italian soft black leather shoes, and a charcoal button-down shirt with a bolo tie. Not only that, but his hair was spiked up like the lead singer of a boy band. "Oh, thanks a lot!" said Billy.

"What? You don't like it?" asked Suzy between giggles.

"I look like—" but he couldn't finish his simile, as he was stunned by Suzy's makeover. She wore a ball gown suitable for a princess. Silvery silk covered in pearls draped from her shoulders to the floor. Billy thought that if she danced, she would ring like a bell. Her hair was up, with matching pearls and ribbons entwined in it. Billy wondered if he'd ever seen her neck and shoulders without her hair, a lab coat, or her father's old shirts over them. For the first time, Billy thought his friend Suzy might be too pretty to talk to. His stammers proved his point.

Suzy wasn't sure what to think of Billy's reaction. She thought he might laugh, tell her how dumb she looked, and say they should get back to work. She thought he might say she looked nice, but they had to get back to work. She thought a lot of things, but she didn't think he'd be speechless. "I figured I'd have a little fun," she said to break the tension.

"Suzy, you're beautiful!"

Those were the right words, but they came from the

wrong person. "Thanks, Mom."

"Ah, yeah," said the right person with the wrong words. "It's fun."

"It was stupid. We have work to do."

"It's fine," said Billy.

"Did you get the wand?" asked Suzy for a second time.

"I'm not certain," said Billy, like it was the cleverest pun ever. "Get it?"

No one did.

"Heisenberg's Uncertainty Principle?"

Nothing.

"Schrodinger's Cat?"

"I've heard of that," said Mrs. Q. "But, I don't know exactly what it means."

"It means," said Billy, "that inside this block of wood, my wand is both there, and not there."

Mrs. Quinofski's blank expression meant he had to explain further.

"The Teacher can read our thoughts, and inside the Quantum World, we have no way of knowing if he is with us or against us."

"He was against us," said Suzy. "Big time!"

"Even so," said Billy, "If I had known for a fact I had the wand, he would never have let us out of there."

"He didn't," said Suzy. "We had to fight our way out."

"I think it would have been worse if he thought we had the wand."

"So why didn't he think that," asked Mrs. Q.

"Because of Schrodinger's Cat," said Billy. "I had my brother, Peter, make a puzzle box with enough room inside to hold my wand. I told him to make it extra hard to solve, and that he shouldn't tell anyone, especially me, how to open it."

"That way no one in the Quantum World would know how to open it either," said Suzy.

"Right," said Billy. "While we were in there, I thought about my wand being in the box, but because of quantum entanglement, I couldn't be certain it was there or not, so neither could the Teacher."

"So you could have the wand," said the General, "and not know you had it at the same time."

"Exactly," said Billy. "All we have to do now is get Peter to open the box."

"After I change," said Suzy — to her mother's disappointment, which was expressed, and Billy's, which was not.

"OPEN IT. ... PLEASE."

Billy handed the puzzle box to Peter, who stood dumbfounded in the doorway of his bedroom. It took him a second to recognize his little brother, as he was dressed like an Italian hipster, accompanied by Suzy, her mother and General-father. The two adults were equally stunned to see Billy's living condition. Sure, he had magically cleaned everything a few months ago, but Billy's mother had begun to stash her new "treasures" in hidden places around the trailer. Billy and Peter were used to the smell, but the Quinofskis were not. They made an unspoken agreement to let Billy spend as much time at their house as he wished, which was a vibe Billy didn't need a magic wand to pick up on.

"Did it work?" Peter asked.

"We're about to find out," said Billy.

Peter flipped the box around, inspecting it closely. When he found what he was looking for, he rubbed a spot near a corner with his thumb. "The trick is the little bit of stickum I put on the wood. It'll take a good rubbing to loosen the key."

"Like Aladdin's Lamp," said Suzy.

"Something like that," said Peter. With some effort, he worked out a piece of wood about as wide as a pencil, but only a couple of inches long. This exposed a hole in the box. Peter used the small piece he had extracted like a key, putting it in the hole. With a push, a part of the puzzle poked out of the other end. From there, Peter quickly manipulated the loosening pieces.

"Is it there?" asked Suzy.

Billy couldn't wait. He snatched the puzzle box from Peter's hands and wedged out the loose pieces. From the light, creamy redwood, Billy pulled the one stick he'd been looking for, his wand. "It's here." He held it up for everyone to see.

"Does it work?" asked the General.

"Let's see," said Billy. He had a clear image in his mind of what he wanted to do, so he didn't have to put it into words. Instead, he thought of what he wanted, and tapped the button.

Poof! A small spark and a puff of smoke popped from the tip of his wand. Other than that, nothing obvious changed.

"Maybe it needs a new battery," said the General.

Billy took in a deep breath. "No, it worked."

Peter did the same. "Fresh air. Nice!"

Now that the brothers brought it up, General Quin-ofski noticed that the mobile home no longer smelled like a garbage dump. "I see what you mean, Billy. Good job."

Mrs. Quinofski couldn't resist the joke of having a magic wand around the house. "Could I borrow that for the rest of the weekend?"

"I wish you could, Mrs. Q," said Billy, "but we have some pressing magic that needs doing."

Ten

BAND ON THE RUN

BEFORE THEY GOT to the pressing magic, the Quinofskis took Billy and Peter to lunch on the base, which was more of a meeting than a social affair. The General arranged for a private dining hall so they could talk without anyone overhearing. Anyone human, that is. Fame jumped up on the window sill and went unnoticed by everyone but Billy and Suzy.

Just as they sat down, Fame shot a thought to both of the kids. *The Teacher says he's sorry.*

Billy had been running the whole morning through his head. *Never mind him, where were you?*

I was doing my part.

How do you figure? Suzy had more than a touch of bitterness *in her thoughts.*

I was running interference, thought Fame. *But the important thing now is to order.*

"What?" asked Suzy out loud.

"What would you like to drink?" asked their waiter, apparently for the second time.

Suzy realized everyone was waiting on her. "Iced tea, thanks."

Billy laughed, "That really is funny."

"What's funny about iced tea?" asked Peter.

"Nothing," said Billy. It was Suzy's turn to giggle.

When the waiter left, General Quinofski spoke up. "Peter, I want to thank you for your help."

Peter's day was turning into a never-ending string of surprises. From having everyone show up for the opening of the box, to lunch, and now a thank you from the most important man in town — and possibly a lot more important than that. Peter wasn't sure what to say. "Anything for Billy," finally came out of his mouth.

Billy let that comment slide, but mentally filed it away for future use.

"I want to make a couple of things clear," said the General. "First, anything to do with their wands is classified. You can't tell anyone."

"Believe me, sir," said Billy. "Peter doesn't want anyone to know we're related, so I wouldn't worry around that."

"Does the thing really work?" asked Peter. "I mean, I've seen Billy do tricks with it that make Mom think he can keep away evil gnomes." His tone made it clear he thought yard gnomes were just little lifeless statues. "And, you know, a little air-freshener shooting out of the tip is easy."

"I used it to clean the house last year," said Billy.

"Really?"

Billy shrugged in a way that said, how else?

Peter turned to the General. "Top secret, got it."

"The second thing," said the General. "Now that my memory has cleared up, I recall that our wand build teams couldn't make a working prototype. I was wondering if there was anything, I don't know, tricky, you did with the wood."

"Nothing tricky," said Peter. "Just a lot of careful work."

I might have an answer to that, thought Fame. *We're working on the same problem.*

"Hang on, Dad," said Suzy. "Billy might have an idea about that." Then she thought, *Go Fame.*

We believe that in order for a wand to work, the user has to have some kind of connection with our side.

What kind of connection?

Like an invitation. We're still trying to figure out the details.

Billy explained to his human company. "In talking with our quantum friend, they think that a person has to have some kind of connection with the Quantum World. Without that, the wand will never work."

"So you're saying some people are witches and warlocks and others aren't?" asked Peter.

"It seems so."

Suzy said to Billy with the deepest British accent she could muster, "You're a wizard, Billy."

Billy grinned. "That's the worst Hagrid imitation I've ever heard." Everyone laughed. "Besides," he tried his own version, "You're a witch, Suzy."

The waiter brought drinks while the laughs died

down. There was a lot of stress to relieve. The General kept things cheery until the waiter left, then he got back down to business.

"Why do you think we all forgot about magic?"

"Isn't it obvious?" The deep, powerful, voice came from thin hair. "Someone has made another wand."

When Suzy saw the Teacher standing next to the open window, she shrieked, jumped out of her chair, and instinctively drew her wand. "What are you doing here?"

Billy drew his wand and stood beside her. Suzy pushed Billy to one side, "Flank him to the left." Apparently, her father had taught her the basics of his line of work.

The Teacher held his hands out in a peaceful way. "I'm sorry." Billy and Suzy held their ground. When they did not advance, the Teacher went on. "That's all the time for apologies. Now that you have your wand back, they will stop at nothing to get another one."

"Will someone tell me what's happening?" asked Peter. No one did.

"Not just your wand, Billy," said the Teacher, "but Suzy's as well. And there is a third."

Outside, storm clouds gathered in a dark plume. In seconds, they blocked the sun. A crack of lightning shattered the window just as Fame jumped to safety.

"Run, Billy!" shouted the Teacher over the wail of wind that blew shards of glass and wood around the room.

"Come on!" said Billy. He grabbed Suzy and they headed for the door, but the Teacher blocked their way. "No, run like a wizard! Take them with you."

Billy acted out of instinct. He pressed the button on his wand, whipped a jet of white-energy over his head like a rope, lassoed the humans in the room, and yanked them toward the safest place he knew.

An instant later, Billy, Peter, Suzy and her parents appeared in Suzy's biology lab in the Quinofski's basement. The transition was so fast that they all fell to the floor, as their muscles were still fighting a massive wind that was no longer there.

"Oh my god, what just happened?" asked Peter.

Before anyone could answer, Fame appeared in her human form. "Billy, not here. They'll find you in a heartbeat. You have to go somewhere no one would ever expect you and Suzy to be."

Fame noticed that, rather than shouting out potential hiding places, everyone was just staring at her. She looked down at herself to see her human form. "Oops." She waved to everyone with an embarrassed smile. "Hi." She disappeared, but reminded Billy and Suzy to *Run!*

Billy repeated his lasso trick. He didn't have time to think of a specific destination, so he thought about going somewhere no one would ever expect to find him.

THE SCREAM THAT MET THEM when they landed nearly blew out their eardrums. "What are you doing here?"

"Yeah, this is pretty much the last place I'd expect to find Billy," said Peter. Then to the girl who screamed, "Hi, Linda."

"What is going on?" Linda stood in her basement family room, wearing a long old T-shirt and wool socks. She had her cell phone in one hand and a pint of ice cream in the other. Clearly, she wasn't expecting visitors to pop in.

Billy wasn't sure how a dating couple should greet each other, but he didn't think Peter's sheepish step back and glance down at the floor was typical, even under these crazy circumstances.

Suzy's body language literacy was light years more advanced than Billy's. "Are you two okay?" she whispered to Peter.

"Define okay."

"Now you're sounding like Billy," she said. Peter gave her a there's-your-answer kind of smirk.

Meanwhile, General Quinofski calmly took Linda's phone. She was shocked to the point of petrification, so she didn't question his actions. The General spoke into the phone. "I'm sorry. Linda will have to call you back." He listened for a second. "No, she's fine. She'll talk to you tomorrow. Have a nice weekend." He pressed the red button on the phone and handed it back to her. "He sounds like a nice young man. Tell him your father came home early and was upset about your chores not being done."

"Peter," asked Linda, "who are these people?"

"Forget about them. Who was the 'nice young man' you were talking to?"

Billy recognized Peter's sarcastic tone and stepped in before they went way off topic. "Linda, hi. Sorry for the intrusion. It's kind of a long story about why we are here, but your magic spell for my calculus test worked." He showed her the novelty toy in his hand. "And so does my magic wand."

Before she could think why she was doing it, Linda

jumped back. "Get that thing away from me, you nearly killed me last time you... wait." Her gaze went distant and her jaw stopped in mid-speech.

"Those are memories," said Billy. "You're going to feel really weird for a while."

General Quinofski checked his phone as he said, "Peter, could you help her with her memories?"

"Yes, sir."

"Billy, Suzy, you're with me." The General stepped to a far corner of the small finished basement and talked on his phone, while Mrs. Quinofski gave the kids a quick hug.

"Hi, it's me," said the General on his phone. "Listen, a freak tornado... oh, you saw it. Is anyone hurt?... Good. Reports are going to come out that my family and I, along with some friends, were having lunch in the private room that was destroyed. That's true. We're fine. No one is hurt, but the kids are a little shaken up, so we are calming down out of the spotlight, okay?... Good. Spread the word, and call me if there's anymore ... weather." He hung up his phone and asked Billy, "Where are we?"

"Linda Lubinski's house."

"Her name sounds familiar."

Suzy said, "She's one of the coven of witches that Billy nearly blew up last year."

"Right," said her father. "She's also heading up the sit-in, yes?"

"Yeah," said Billy. "Her and a few others."

"So why wouldn't anyone expect to find you here?"

Billy blushed. Suzy answered. "Because, Billy has a

big crush on her, but she's dating his brother and thinks Billy and I are dorks — at least, up until recently with the protest and everything."

"Well, your quantum friends haven't dropped by, so I assume we're safe for now, but we can't hide forever."

Mrs. Quinofski asked, "How are they able to follow us?"

"I'm not sure," said Billy, "but probably the same way I got us here. I didn't think of coming here, I thought of going where no one would expect to find me. Somehow the wand picks up on what I'm actually thinking."

"Or feeling," added Suzy.

The General crossed his arms and sighed. "So they can find you just by thinking about you."

"I guess," said Billy.

"But apparently," said the General, "there are ways to hide from their thoughts, otherwise there would be a tornado over this house right now."

Peter had been listening. He offered a suggestion. "Sounds like you guys need Magneto's helmet."

"Is that like Hector's shiny helmet?" asked Suzy.

"I don't know who that is," said Peter

"Maybe Hades' Helmet of Invisibility?"

"Never heard of it," said Peter.

"Was that on Xena: Warrior Princess?" asked Linda, who was still in a mental blur.

General Quinofski explained Peter's comic book allusion. "Magneto's helmet hides his thoughts from Professor Xavier."

Suzy grunted with a touch of disgust. "X-Men. I should have known." She filled in Billy and the rest. "Dad thinks X-Men should be taught in schools as modern American literature."

"Good idea, G.Q.," said Peter.

"No, you're the one with the good idea," said the General. "Billy, Suzy, do you think you could come up with a spell to make us invisible to the dark quantum beings?"

"A spell!?" asked Linda from the fog that was her brain.

Before anyone could respond, the weather interrupted. The Lubinski house was built on a hill, so their basement had a door and windows on one side. That's how everyone noticed that the outside world suddenly went dark.

"They're here," said Peter in a parody of his favorite horror movie.

"We've got to move," said the General. He pointed to Linda. "Bring her, too."

Lightning flashed.

Billy counted. "One-one thousand, two-one thousand."

A massive crack of thunder shook the entire Lubinski house.

"Twenty-two hundred feet away. I don't think they know where we are."

"Maybe not," said the General, "but they will bomb this neighborhood flat to find us."

Linda had reached her limit. "What is happening?"

Suzy asked, "Billy, where can we go?"

"I have an idea." He didn't bother to explain it. He just fired his wand and took them home.

Catch me if you can.

Billy put that thought out into the world just before he materialized his posse inside his mobile home.

"Billy," said his mom as if he just got home from school. "You brought your friends, how nice."

Billy shot his wand at the ceiling. "*Scutum absconditum.*" The white energy went through the roof. From the windows everyone could see the electric charge cascade down an invisible dome that covered the house.

"Where am I?" asked Linda.

"My house," said Billy.

"How did I get here?"

"Magic."

Suzy couldn't resist. "What's the matter, Linda? Don't you believe in magic?"

General Quinofski looked out of the window at the sky. "The storm is coming this way."

"Yeah," said Billy. "I kind of told them where to find us."

"Why did you do that?" asked Peter.

"I couldn't have them blow up the whole town looking for us. I think we'll be safe under my force field. After all, it's kept the yard gnomes out."

"No way!" said Peter.

"That's true," said Billy's mom. She pointed out the window to the neighbor's yard decorations. "Ever since Billy made his invisible force field, they can look, but they can't come in."

Everyone followed her lead to see a collection of

gnomes and other inanimate yard animals arranged in a semicircle outside of the dome area, all looking their way.

"It's the pink flamingo that really creeps me out," said Peter.

"Wait a minute," said Linda. "Billy, you tried to blow me up. You're wanted by the police and everything."

"That was last year," said Billy, "but welcome back to the real world."

A bolt of lightning with instantaneous thunder hit the dome and harmlessly bounded off into the sky. "Impressive," said the General.

"At least they aren't blowing up Linda's neighborhood," said Suzy.

"Yes," said her father. "That was good quick thinking, Billy. You saved a lot of lives and bought us some time. Now let's work on that Helmet of Invisibility."

Peter saw that Linda was about to ask another question, so he cut her off before she could. "Just go with it. I'll explain later."

"The thing is," said Billy. "I'm not sure I can just say 'Magic Helmet' and expect the wand to do the rest. I have to have some idea how it works."

Another bolt of lightning, like Thor's Hammer, hit the dome. When the noise cleared, Suzy flicked her wand toward the ceiling. "*Immunio scutum absconditum.*" Energy shot out from all parts of her wand to the dome. She then said to the room, "A little fortification never hurt."

Her father stayed on point. "How do they read our thoughts?"

Suzy answered. "Thoughts are electrical impulses,

Dad. They are real, tangible things. Our brains all —
probably — radiate a unique electrical signature. These
quantum life forms could see our electrical fields the
same way we see faces."

"You're talking about auras," said Linda.

"That could be," said Suzy. She expected Billy to
chime in, but he just sat on the couch with his fist to his
lips, rocking back and forth. In other words, thinking.

Billy spoke to his knuckles. "We can't just block out
everyone. There are some quantum beings we need on
our side. A phase shift could do it, but no one has been
able to do that before."

"What's he talking about?" asked Linda.

"He's trying to figure out scientifically how to hide
your aura," said Suzy.

Linda didn't pick up the "shush" tone in Suzy's
answer. "What's a phase shift?"

Billy suddenly joined the conversation. "Everything in
reality vibrates at a certain frequency, or, uh… um… like
a movie, it's twenty-four frames per second, right? Well, if
the projector flashes every twenty-four frames, and you
hide in every other frame, then no one would ever see
you unless the projector was recalibrated to either forty-
eight frames per second, or … or, or, or, you know, uh,
twenty-four frames a second but starting on your frame
and not theirs. That makes sense, right?"

"I thought movies were digital," said Linda.

"They are, it's just a model. Or a theory. I don't know,
maybe it's complete science-fiction. I don't know the difference anymore."

Suzy had never heard him go off the rails like this. "Billy, are you okay?"

"No." He didn't look it, either. He'd broken out in a cold sweat, and his eyes couldn't focus on any one thing for long. Another crack of lightning made him jump out of his seat. "I'm thirteen years old and half the universe is outside trying to kill me. The other half says that I'm responsible for the world's problems and have to find a solution. I don't know what to do!"

Billy shook uncontrollably. In full meltdown, all he could do was dive into his mother's arms for comfort. There he repeated his worst nightmare. "I don't know what to do."

"Billy, it's simple." Fame had joined them, but this time she wasn't a cat or a tomboy. She was the Lady of the Lake. She had long, glowing blonde hair, held back by a simple gold band. She wore a gossamer-white gown and appeared in a ball of light that shimmered between pure white and the hues of a summer sunrise.

Her appearance instilled a euphoric calm in everyone. "Nothing is more powerful than your imagination," she said. "Trust it."

Billy looked at his wand, then to Suzy.

"What have you got to lose?" she said.

He looked to Fame in her new form, but she had vanished.

Another crack of lightning and thunder ripped against their shield. Billy held up his wand and said, "Phase shift." He pressed the button.

A stream of energy bounced off the ceiling, split into

seven pieces and buzzed around the head of each mortal.

Once they dissipated, Mrs. Quinofski asked the question on everyone's mind. "Did it work?"

General Quinofski whispered, "Don't look out the window. Don't move."

"I feel like I'm in a submarine movie," whispered Peter.

The noisy wind outside of the protective dome slowed to a stop, and after a moment, the clouds whisked away. Another full minute of silence followed before everyone broke out in a cheer.

Billy, thought Fame, *it worked. I can't find you anywhere.*

Billy fired his wand in no particular direction and said, "Sync," while thinking of the Teacher and Fame.

There you are. Good work.

"Good work, indeed," said the Teacher, who suddenly stepped out from Billy's bedroom.

"Oh, another guest," said Billy's mother. "Will you all be staying for dinner?"

"No, thank you Mrs. Bobble," said the Teacher in the kindest voice Billy had ever heard from him. "I can't stay." To the others his tone was more serious. "Billy, Suzy, and the rest of you, find the third wand before they get tired of trying to take yours." He turned to Linda. "And continue your fight in the schools, young Miss Lubinski."

"How do you know who I am?"

The Teacher smiled in a way that only wise old men can toward a pretty young girl. "You and your coven have come a long way since last year. Fighting ignorance becomes you." Instead of disappearing as he usually did, the Teacher went out the front door and shooed away the yard gnomes as he walked out of the trailer park.

Inside the trailer, everyone but Billy and his mother marveled at how the little clay statues came to life and ran away in fear from the mysterious old man.

Eleven

Prepare for a Showdown

"I AM KIND OF HUNGRY," said Suzy when the dust had settled.

"Well," said Billy's Mom, "I can whip something up real quick if you like."

"Trust me," said Peter, "You don't want to eat here."

"Mrs. Bobble," said General Quinofski, "Our lunch was rudely interrupted, so I think we might go back to our house and order in. Would you like to join us?"

"Oh no," she said. "I shouldn't leave the house. They might find a way in and do who knows what. I had better hold down the fort here. And I already ate."

"Fair enough. Peter, Linda, join us."

"I don't know, General, sir," said Linda. "My parents are out of town and…"

"It's not exactly a request," said the General. "You are

now privy to a top secret military operation. That gives me the power to... buy you a very nice lunch and insist that you join us."

Linda tugged at her T-shirt to see if it might work as a dress. "Can I get some clothes?"

"Billy?" said the General.

"Dad! Uh ... no." Suzy pointed her wand toward Linda. "I always liked you in this outfit." Suzy fired her wand and Linda had an instant gothic makeover — complete with hair and makeup.

Linda looked at her flowing black clothes. "Wow, I never thought you noticed."

Suzy eyed the two Bobble boys. "I'm not the only one." She then had to state the obvious. "It's a good look for you."

"Thanks, Suzy." Linda made eye contact with Suzy. "Really. Thank you."

Suzy blushed a little and broke their gaze. "Sure. Anytime."

The General got them back on schedule. "Billy, could you put us in our living room."

"I think Suzy should do it," said Billy. "She could use the practice."

"Hey, I just made the whole ensemble," said Suzy, like she was about to argue against Billy's observation, but after a second she said, "Okay, you're right, I have a lot of catching up to do. But it's not a bad thing." She raised her wand with confidence, but when she saw everyone waiting to see her do magic, she hesitated. "That's a lot of people."

"We're no different than the furniture," said Billy.

"You have to gather us up, move us to your living room, and let us go. All in one tap."

"Gather and move," said Suzy. "Stick and move. I like that." She adjusted her fingers on her wand, then said to Billy, "You have your wand ready, right? You know, in case we get lost."

"I'm ready."

"Okay." Suzy raised her wand. "Stick and move!" She whipped her wand down and fired.

"Well, we're here," said Billy.

"Good job, honey," said Mrs. Quinofski

"Yeah," said Peter, "and we're stuck all right."

Sure enough, Suzy had stuck everyone together in a big group hug, which no one could seem to get out of. They stood cheek-to-cheek, unable to move from where they stood in Suzy's living room.

"Suzy," said Billy, "try saying, 'oops,' and tapping your wand."

The instant everyone was unstuck, they lost what little balance they had and fell to the floor.

"Sorry about that," said Suzy.

All was forgiven, and the rest of lunch was uneventful. The conversation was mostly a complete explanation of the history of Billy and Suzy's creation of the wands. This started for Linda's sake but ended up helping everyone else put together their jigsaw-puzzle memories. That was followed by a re-cap of what had happened on the most recent trip into the Quantum World. The part about the black smoke of Death coming toward them prompted Mrs. Quinofski's concern. "You said this wasn't dangerous."

"Crossing the street is dangerous, Mrs. Q.," said Billy. "It's all a matter of perspective."

Peter thought being sneezed out of an old man's nose was a fate worse than death, but overall he was impressed with his little brother. "I had no idea this stuff was real. I mean, you know, really real, right?"

"It's crazy," said Linda. "Billy, you always said we were nuts for believing in magic, but this… this is crazy."

"It is crazy," said the General. "It is also real, and dangerous. I wish this responsibility hadn't fallen on your shoulders, kids. You're way too young for this."

"Tell me about it," said Billy. Then he corrected himself. "I didn't mean that. I mean, we can handle it, sir. I'm sorry for the way I acted back at my house."

"No apology necessary, soldier. If my mother had been around, I think I'd have done the same thing. This is scary stuff."

"Yeah, Dad. It's scary, sure, but we don't exactly have a choice."

"Agreed," said the General. "So let's see if we can't figure this out. We have Billy's wand back, but we never figured out why we all forgot it existed?"

"The Teacher said there's another wand," said Suzy.

"How many have you two made?" asked her father.

"The two that work and the one that didn't," said Billy.

"I can't imagine that's the other wand," said Suzy.

Her father didn't seem to think so either. "Did you tell anyone else about how to make a wand?"

"Nobody else would understand it," said Suzy.

Billy asked, "What about all of the scientists you brought on to Operation Hocus Pocus?"

Peter snorted. "Really? Who came up with that lame name?"

Billy, Suzy, and her mom all pointed to the General.

"It's brilliant, G.Q.," said Peter.

General Quinofski ignored him. "I'll have to look into those scientists." He made a note on his phone. "Anyone else?"

"Yeah," said Billy. "There was…" but he couldn't think of anyone. "No, wait, I guess not."

Suzy joined in. "No, you're right, Billy. There was that guy."

"What guy?"

"I don't know, Dad. Mom, you told me about him, I think."

"I did?"

"I don't know," said Suzy. "Maybe I made it up."

"Maybe not," said Billy. "Someone messed with our memories before. They could have done it again."

LINDA WAS ASLEEP by the time Billy zapped her home. General Quinofski didn't think she'd keep their secret for long, even with the threat of a treason charge he'd made very clear. Suzy managed to say between yawns that Linda might tell the rest of her coven, but no one else — and no one would believe them if they told, so the secret should be safe for a while.

Shortly after that conversation, fatigue hit the kids hard and heavy. Billy and Suzy were zombies. The General, who knew a thing or two about fighting for one's life, reassured them. "The adrenaline has worn off. You're about to sleep long and deep."

When Billy said he was okay to walk home, Peter didn't have much choice but to join him. Billy was surprised he didn't come up with an excuse to have to be somewhere else.

Once they were out of everyone's earshot, Peter got chatty. "So you really did all of that stuff?"

"What? You think I made it up?"

"No, I didn't say that."

"You think I couldn't do something cool?"

"Relax, Wild Brain Bill, it wasn't a dig. I just... I don't know. I guess I'm proud of you."

Billy didn't know what to say, so they walked for a couple of more steps before he came out with, "Thanks." Then it was Peter's turn not to know what to say. They walked a little more before Billy changed the subject. "There's something you should know about Mom."

"That's she's crazy? Yeah, I know."

"Actually, she's not," said Billy. "I mean, she is from our point of view, but in fact she's tapped into the Quantum World. The voices she hears, the yard gnomes she's afraid of, those things are all real."

"You think?"

Billy misunderstood his brother's response and got defensive. "Why do you always think I'm making things up?"

"I meant, 'you think?' like, 'duh, I saw the yard gnomes.' Why do you take things so literally?"

"It's sort of what I do," said Billy.

"Well, stop it, would you?"

"Sorry."

"What were we talking about?"

"Mom. Suzy thinks that schizophrenia, Alzheimer's, and autism are all disorders where a person's DNA gets knocked out of synch with our timeline. The wand does the same thing, but on a larger scale."

"So the yard gnomes…?"

"They are lesser beings of the Quantum World."

"You mean like squirrels or something?"

"Yeah, sure, I guess — or maybe more like the chimpanzees that can do sign language. I don't know. Anyway, Mom can see them in their time-space continuum."

"Like when they ran away from that old guy."

"Yeah. She see them that way all the time."

"She always says they are after her baby," said Peter.

"She's not wrong. They've been keeping an eye on me from day one."

"When I was little, I used to wonder why they weren't after me. Like Mom didn't care about me."

"Well, now you know the truth. Mom cared. It was the Quantum yard gnomes that didn't."

"Thanks. You saved me years of therapy."

"You never struck me as the therapy sort," said Billy.

"Speaking of which, does all of this getting your memory back mean you don't have to get therapy anymore?"

Billy stopped dead in his tracks.

"What?" asked Peter.

"I know who has the other wand."

"BILLY, SO GLAD to see you," said Billy, mocking Dr. Menaus's voice. He played out the scene for Peter as they headed home. "That's what he told me when I showed up at school."

At least Peter was headed straight home. Billy pinged in one direction then ponged in another. He would stop, remember, get angry, run in a circle, and then start toward home again. Peter began to feel like he was walking a hyperactive dog.

"He said to me, 'Let's talk, shall we?' Then he leads me to his office like we're the best of friends."

"Who did? Who are you talking about?" asked Peter.

"Dr. Menaus, at Oakridge Academy."

"The one you beat up?"

"Yeah." Billy didn't bother with details of the fight, not yet. "His first memory spell—" He interrupted his own thought and stopped walking. "I've got to figure out how he did that." He started walking again. "The first spell didn't take. Not for me. I remembered everything, or it came back to me, like now. I don't know; doesn't matter. The point is, I figured out that he must have been the one who erased everyone's memory, so I confronted him."

"Bad move, little brainer. You should have gotten help."

"I tried! But everyone thought I was crazy."

"Yeah, I could see that."

"He knew I knew. I tried to hide it, but I couldn't. When we got to his office I told him I knew he'd made a wand. I watched him closely. I figured he'd try to use his wand on me. I kept my eyes peeled for something up his sleeve, or a wand on his desk. I didn't count on a five-foot staff. He got to it before I did, and that's when the fight started."

"Fighting isn't your strong suit."

"Yeah well, it's not his either, but he's a lot bigger

than I am. He got the staff and used his memory spell before I could stop him. I kept fighting, but I didn't know why anymore. All I knew was that I was angry. Then I was arrested."

"So what are you going to do about it?"

Billy smiled. "Get a little help from my friends."

BILLY CALLED SUZY'S land line the minute he and Peter got home. He knew Suzy would be asleep, so she wouldn't answer her cell. No matter, it was her Dad he needed to talk to.

"We're going to have to get the local police involved," was General Quinofski's first thought about Dr. Menaus. After a bit of silence, he continued. "Tomorrow is Sunday, Billy. I want you to rest. If you're half as tired as Suzy is, you'll need it. I have the surveillance tapes from Suzy's deposition, so I'll use that on the detectives the way you did me and ask them to keep an eye on Dr. Menaus."

"They have to be careful," said Billy. "He can't know we've remembered, or the whole thing will start over again."

"I understand, son."

"For all we know, we've had this conversation a hundred times before."

"If that's the case," said the General, "I think this time it will be different."

"I hope so."

"Put it out of your mind for a day, Billy. Relax. Watch some football. Janice tells me you all are in for a big day at school on Monday. We'll debrief after that, okay?"

"Okay, sir." Billy hung up.

Fame, as a cat, jumped onto his bed. *Are you all right?*

"Yeah." Billy figured he could talk out loud since no one else was around.

Anything I can do?

"No, I don't think—" Billy got an idea, but he wasn't sure it would work. "Fame, can I ask you something?"

She jumped off the bed and grew into her human tomboyish self. "About the Lady of the Lake outfit? I figured you needed some kind of big, dramatic inspiration."

"Thanks, but that's not what I was going to ask. I know who has the other wand. Does that mean you know, too?"

"No, you've got it pretty well blocked in your head. The Teacher could probably pry it out of you, but I don't have his skills."

"If I have you keep an eye on the guy who has it, can I trust you not to turn into one of them, like the Teacher did?"

"Here's the thing about that." She sat on Billy's desk with her feet in his chair. "In this world, thoughts stay thoughts. I can daydream all I want about the kind of power a wand would bring, and still be true to my word not to do anything against your wishes."

"What about when you go back home?"

Fame thought about it for the length of a sigh. "Then it's harder to control." When Billy pursed his lips, she clarified. "But this other wand is in your world. I would have to come here to get it. When I did, my head would clear and I'd be all, 'Duh, that was stupid.'"

Billy didn't crack a smile. "That's why it was so dangerous having my wand in your world."

"Yeah, pretty much."

Billy looked at the floor. "Even the Teacher couldn't control himself."

Fame got up to inspect Billy's pristine-to-the-point-of-being-Spartan room. "I don't know about that."

"What do you mean? He tried to kill me."

"Did he?"

"Yes!"

"Billy, if the Teacher wanted to kill you, you'd be dead."

"But we saw the black smoke, like before. And you said that was Death."

"It is. You saw the black smoke of death, and then you saw the Teacher, who did a feeble job of trying to kill you."

"Feeble?!"

"You saw the smoke of death, then the Teacher, so you think he sent it."

"You mean he didn't?"

"I don't know, Billy. He might have. I do know that he plays games, very dangerous games, with everyone."

"Why does he do that?"

"I don't know that either. But more often than not, if you play his games, you come out the winner."

"If you live."

"Another thing to keep in mind, Billy. Your wand was in our world for a long time by our standards. Sure, that has made for some bad things happening here, but the Teacher and I fought to keep the others from punching a whole between our worlds and bringing a reign of terror for centuries, so give us some credit."

Billy thought for a moment, then got back to his original idea. "Okay. I need you to keep an eye on someone."

"Great! I love being a spy!"

"HE'S HAD A VISITOR."

Fame reported to Suzy and Billy at the trailer park's playground on Sunday afternoon.

"Yeah, who?" asked Billy.

"No one good. He's the Teacher's counterpart. Where the Teacher is part of the collective consciousness of a wise, old, father figure – this guy gets his power from human fear and paranoia."

"What did they talk about?" asked Suzy.

"They said if Menaus can't get your wands, then they will take his."

"Great," said Billy. "Someone else that wants to kill us."

Fame tried to lighten the mood. "You should see the inside of his house. He's given himself all kinds of luxuries, but as far as I can tell, has kept the outside unchanged."

"He's probably worried about the IRS," said Suzy.

"He's put a shimmer on his car," Fame said.

"A shimmer?" asked Suzy.

Billy answered. "That's from *Dr. Who. Reboot Season 4: The End of Time – Part One*. A shimmer is what the aliens wear to disguise themselves as humans."

Fame explained to Suzy. "I have to use science-fictions terms since Billy doesn't know the first thing about the history or practice of magic."

Suzy and Fame giggled. Billy got them back on subject. "So he's disguising his car."

"Yeah it's really a Lamborghini Veneno," said Fame. "He has it disguised as a Nissan Ultima."

"He's afraid someone will notice he's using magic," said Billy.

"Obviously," said Suzy. "So what does that mean to us?"

"I don't know. Maybe it's something we can use against him later."

"You say that like it's going to come to a showdown," said Suzy.

"What makes you think it's not? He's not going to let anyone walk in there and take his magic away. We're going to have to fight magic with magic, and besides him, the only other witches and wizards in the world are you and me."

Twelve

COMMUNICATION BREAKDOWN

"SHOULD I TAKE my wand to school?" Suzy texted to Billy just before seven o'clock the next morning. "Absolutely," he answered. He started to elaborate but got tired of typing with his thumbs, so he thought, *Fame, tell Suzy how important it is for her to have her wand with her at all times.*

A few seconds later, Fame filled his thoughts: *She gets it, and wants to know if you're watching the news.*

Tell her I have it on now.

"Pandemonium is the only way to describe it," said a local reporter on TV. "Advocacy groups on both sides of the issue have bussed in supporters from all over the country. Meanwhile, students, teachers, and administrators have remained inside the school as part of the sit-in protest."

Suzy said her mom wants to know if you want a ride to school.

Tell her, sure.

You guys know about cell phones, right? Or do I have to relay every thought all day long? And stop giggling, it tickles!

TURNS OUT, THE RIDE to school might not have been the best idea.

"You know, we could, uh, use our own mode of transportation." From the backseat of a military Humvee, Billy indicated the wand up his sleeve to Suzy, meaning they could magically transport themselves past the crowds. He knew how much Suzy hated going to school in a Hummer, but her mom thought it would be the best way to go given the protestors, so she ordered a driver from the base.

The streets leading up to Winston High were lined with chartered busses. Traffic was at a standstill, as parents trying to drop off their kids yelled at the gathering crowds. Billy and Suzy counted nine different state license plates of the few they could see. There were also news vans parked in every imaginable space. Suzy recognized the call letters and some of the reporters from local channels. Their vans had microwave antennas raised high in the air. A handful of bigger trucks with national network logos had satellite dishes attached. Billy would have given anything to spend some time in one of those, bouncing signals around the planet, but the protestors soon brought him back to their strange reality.

He noticed that some of the protestors wore head-sets. They barked at the others as they got off of their busses. Billy did some fundamental lip-reading, "Get moving," and "Over there."

"Mrs. Q?" he asked. "Who are the people with the headsets yelling at everyone?"

"Organizers," she said. "They like to say these things are grassroots and spontaneous, but it takes a lot of behind-the-scenes work to get a mob of these nut-jobs together to parade in front of the cameras."

"Mom!" Suzy was surprised by her mother's language. Normally she wouldn't say a bad thing about anyone. Suzy figured the traffic jam was getting to her and giggled. "Can I quote you on that?"

"Not if you ever want to come home again." She was kidding. She didn't sound like she was, but Suzy knew she wasn't in trouble.

Billy watched the organizers herd their charges together, and couldn't help but think how they resembled the Quantum beings, manipulating people into taking actions — good and bad. He hoped the people in the crowd had stopped to think about what they were doing. That their participation was part of free will and not blind allegiance.

He also wondered if he was being handled by the Teacher.

"There she is!" Someone in the crowd pointed at the Humvee. Mobs for… whatever they were for, and against the same thing… raced toward the vehicle that was hopelessly stuck in traffic. In seconds, they were surrounded.

Some chanted, "Su-ZEE! Su-ZEE!" while others shouted angry, rude things.

"Ma'am?" The sergeant driving the Humvee was a tough young woman. Billy figured she could have driven them out of anything if ordered not to worry about running over people and cars. This crisis wasn't that bad… yet.

A call came over the car's radio. The sergeant responded. "Roger, we are stuck in traffic and surrounded by hostiles."

That made Billy wonder. Were they all hostile?

"Negative," said the sergeant in the radio. "Cargo appears safe at the moment."

"Great," said Suzy. "Now we're cargo."

"Is that your dad?" asked Billy.

"Yeah, he's either watching us on the news or over some unmanned drone that's not supposed be flying in the U.S."

"Ask him if we can use Hocus Pocus."

"Mom?"

"Didn't we have enough of that on Saturday?" said Mrs. Quinofski.

"At least you know we're good at it," said Billy.

Mrs. Quinofski put her hand out to the driver for her headset. "Sergeant?"

The sergeant smiled and pressed a button the steering wheel. "You're on speaker."

Mrs. Quinofski spoke into the air. "Boss Two, Boss One."

The General's voice came in clear. "Go, Boss One."

"Cargo wants to use Hocus Pocus."

"Can they keep it quiet?"

"Absolutely," said Billy.

Mrs. Quinofski relayed the message. "They say yes."

"It can't hurt to practice, but it's your call, Boss One."

"Copy that. Boss One, out."

Billy asked Suzy, "Where'd your mom learn how to talk like that?"

Mrs. Quinofski answered for her. "U.S. Army colonel, retired."

"How did you think they met?" said Suzy.

Mrs. Quinofski spoke to the driver again. "Sergeant, would you mind stepping out to ask one of the officers how long this might take?"

"Yes, ma'am." The sergeant didn't question what was clearly a request to leave them alone. She simply stepped out of the vehicle.

"Okay, you two, make it quick," said Mrs. Quinofski.

"Take off your coats and block the windows," said Billy.

Mrs. Q draped her coat between the backseat and the front. Suzy held up hers over her window with one hand. Billy did the same, and both kids took out their wands.

"Stoners' Row?" he asked.

"What?!" asked Mrs. Q.

"Sure," said Suzy.

"Best let me drive," said Billy. "I know a trick to make sure no one can see us when we land." He held out his arm so Suzy could hang on to him.

Suzy took it. "Bye, Mom."

"Text me when you land so I know you made it."

"Sure thing, Mrs. Q," said Billy. He pressed the button on his wand, and in a split second the kids and their coats faded from existence without a sound.

"DO YOU SEE ANYONE?"

Billy's landing trick was to get to Stoner's Row at the speed of thought, then tune in the Quantum World enough to get an outline of anyone that might be there.

Suzy answered Billy's question with a question. "What would they look like?"

"I'm not sure completely, but probably like chalk outlines of people."

"Wait!" said Suzy. "There's one right on top of you, or mixed in with you, or something."

"Oh, that's wild, I see it on you, too."

"Should we call it an 'it'? I mean, it's a guy or girl, right?"

"Hard to tell, it's moving around so much. Hang on, I want to dial up my perception a bit."

From past experience, Billy had gotten pretty good at adjusting the balance between the Quantum World and the Human World by picturing a TV contrast control. At this low level, only basic outlines of the regular world were visible. If he let in the whole of the Quantum World, his mind would be completely blown as all of space and all of time presented themselves as separate particle-like things. For now, he edged up perception the tiniest bit.

"Stop!" said Suzy. "Gross, gross, gross!"

"What?"

"It's not one person, it's two. And they are making out!"

"I still can't see them."

"I don't have to see them," said Suzy. "We are occupying the same space at the same time. Linda and Charles are making out and I'm part of them! Gross! Gross! Gross!"

"Linda and Charles?" asked Billy.

"Get me out of here!"

BAM! They weren't at school anymore but in a gritty mechanic's shop in a bad part of a bad neighborhood. Billy must have accidentally let go of the button, because they were fixed in standard time and space.

"What in the world?"

"Hi Peter," said Billy.

Sure enough, Peter pulled his head out from under a hood to find out what blew up, only to see his little brother and Suzy standing in his shop. What could he say but, "Hi."

"Hi Peter," said Suzy with a little wave.

"We got a little lost on our way to school," said Billy.

"How did you end up here?" asked Peter. "You've never been here before."

"It's a long story. Is anyone else here?"

"No. I came in early to catch up on some work."

"Great," said Billy. He was holding Suzy's hand, so he held up his wand. "Don't tell anyone you saw us, okay?"

"Not a problem."

Billy pressed the button on his wand, and again, he and Suzy disappeared in a silent split-second fade.

"I TOTALLY UNDERSTOOD THAT."

Billy held a finger to his mouth and whispered, "Yeah, I thought you might." He had landed them behind the dumpsters outside of the cafeteria. He peeked to see that no one was nearby. "Did you notice I've cut out the sonic booms on take offs and landings?"

"Not really." Suzy was anxious to get away from the smell of the dumpsters.

"Yeah," said Billy. "You have to think about a quick fade out, like a half-second, instead of popping in and out. That gives the atmosphere time to adjust, so no sonic booms."

"Great. I'll remember that." She said it like this was one of Billy's wild ideas that she only half listens to.

"Suzy," said Billy to get her attention. "Do remember that, okay? It might be important someday."

"Okay. I'm sorry. But, between the wild mob out front, becoming one with Linda and Charles, then landing in Peter's garage, and now here, I'm a little freaked out, all right?"

"All right," said Billy. "Let's get out of here. It stinks."

"You're just noticing that?"

Billy mocked her sarcasm by imitating her. "'You're just noticing that?'"

Suzy ignored the dig. "What happened with that air-freshener spell you did?"

"What am I going to tell Peter?"

"Do you think Linda told Charles about Saturday?"

"MAGIC," SAID BILLY when everyone asked how they got through the crowds so quickly. He figured the greatest thing about the truth being so absurd was that no one would believe it, so why lie?

Charles came running into the cafeteria to join the

rest of the negotiation team. "Where is your mom?" he asked Suzy. She didn't answer, but noticed Linda sneaking in after him.

"She's stuck in traffic," said Billy. "Why?"

"She used to run the school board, so everyone seems to think she can come up with a compromise."

"So that's why she was on the phone all day yesterday," said Suzy.

"Speaking of phones," said Billy, "you forgot to text her to say we made it."

From the front door of the cafeteria came a tone that could only be made by an angry parent. "Don't bother." It was Mrs. Quinofski, out of breath, storming into the room. "I ran all the way here."

"Mom! You shouldn't have done that. You're way too old to be running and stuff."

Suzy's mom pointed straight at her. "You and I need to talk. Later. About some rules with that new toy of yours."

"Great," said Suzy under her breath to Billy. "Now everyone thinks I still play with toys."

"It's better than what Linda plays with," said Billy, thinking of his brother's heart.

"So it's settled then?"

Mrs. Quinofski had an agreement within reach, so long as no one got cold feet. She went through the bullet points one more time. "Ms. Fuller will be reinstated. The old textbooks will be used along with the new ones. Teachers and students will be encouraged to discuss the differences between the two versions. Footage from the security cameras will be kept on the school's servers under dual password security. The school board will have one password and the teachers' union the other. Only if both groups are in agreement, or under a subpoena, can the footage be used."

They were so close. Then one of the federal school board members asked, "What about punishment for the students involved in the sit-in?"

The room erupted in debate. First the student representatives lashed out. "Punishment for what? Doing the right thing?"

Then Dillon got defensive about his territorial rights. "Discipline is a matter for each school, not the feds."

And the fight was on.

Billy's mind started to wander until he noticed the Teacher, wearing a tweed suit like something from the early 1900s, sitting in a chair against the wall. Billy caught Suzy's eye and subtly pointed to the Teacher.

The Teacher waved his hand and everyone but Billy and Suzy froze in time. He stood and surveyed the participants, most of whom were captured in the middle of an angry shout. "Are you listening?" he asked the kids, but didn't wait for an answer. "Are you seeing what's happening? One group doesn't trust another group with dispensing punishment on a third group, who feel that what they did was for the greater good. Who is right? Who is wrong?"

It felt like he wanted an answer. "I don't know," said Billy.

"Oh, but you have to know. As you said, Suzy, you two are witches and wizards now. You have the final word over so many things. That stick you have up your sleeve, Billy, and the one in your back pack, Suzy, end all arguments."

He raised his fists to the air and said in a booming voice, "You have power!" He then looked at the kids like he said something hilarious and expected a laugh.

Billy and Suzy stared back at him with eyes as big as saucers. Clearly, the Teacher had lost his mind.

"Sorry," said the Teacher. He practically mumbled. "That was from a cartoon from before your time." Just as quickly, he got back to the point. "What you are seeing here," he indicated the frozen argument in front of them, "is the way Evil works. It can be subtle, like it is here, or obvious like mindless terrorism."

Suzy considered this for a moment. She'd never really thought much about Good vs. Evil. On a day-to-day basis, the subject doesn't come up very much. Now that she and Billy had access to magic, however, that would change. She realized that little decisions made throughout a normal day had elements of Good and Evil. She hoped she'd know which was which when it came time for big decisions.

The Teacher asked "Any questions?"

Clearly, he was asking about his current lesson, but Billy brought it back to physics. "Are you freezing time all over the universe, or just in this room?"

"Who says I froze time?" From his tone, Suzy got the feeling the Teacher wasn't happy with Billy's change of subject. "Maybe I sped us up."

With that, the Teacher was gone. A rush of noise knocked the kids' heads back as the shouting that had been silenced exploded back into the air. Billy and Suzy exchanged an unspoken did-you-see-what-I-saw question.

Call me crazy, thought Fame into each of their heads, *but I'd say the Teacher expects you two to take some action here.*

"Say something," Billy told Suzy.

"What good would that do? No one can hear me."

Billy couldn't deny that logic. Everyone was talking, no one was listening. The noise was unbearable. Suzy tried to get their attention. "Excuse me! Hey! I have something to say!" Nothing worked.

While Suzy ran around shushing people, or waving her arms to try to get them to focus, Billy worked on a problem that had been bugging him for some time. He decided to ask for Fame's help. How did Dr. Menaus use magic to make people forget?

How should I know? she answered. I don't know how your wand works.

Up to that point, Billy had used the wand mostly to transport himself. Last year, he had defended himself in school by inflating some physical faults in bullies who were attacking him. He had transported others, created breakfast out of thin air, torn apart a plywood bad guy, but nothing like erasing people's memories.

"Billy!" said Suzy. "I could use some help here."

"I am helping."

"Mumbling to yourself is not helping, Billy."

"I'm thinking!"

"Well, sometimes you think too much."

He wasn't sure he'd heard her right. "What?"

"Less thinking, more doing."

Billy wondered if she was right. Maybe he was over-thinking this thing. If he wanted everyone to shut-up why not think shut-up and use his wand?

For one thing, said Fame inside his head, *you'd have a lot of explaining to do. Plus, what happens if you think them into never being able to talk again?*

You're a big help, thought Billy. *And don't listen in on my thoughts unless I ask you to!*

Sorry.

Billy tried to think of a way to get people to stop talking. He could have them all choke on something, but that could get dangerous. He could make their vocal chords not work, but like Fame said, what if he couldn't change them back? Then an idea popped into his head.

Tell Suzy to stand-by, he thought to Fame.

She's ready.

Billy got a clear image in his head, a parched desert and chapped, dry lips. Under the table he pulled out his wand, whispered, "Thirsty," and pressed the button.

Silence fell as everyone in the room except Suzy reached for a glass of water at the same time. "Finally!" said Suzy, like she knew what she was going to say all this time. She didn't have a clue, but she was going to talk until something made sense.

"So, we are hung up on this idea of punishment." She didn't know the name of the federal school board member who brought up the subject, so she nodded his way. "Why do you feel we need to be punished?"

"Because you broke the rules."

"That's why you think we need to be punished, but why do you feel we should be punished?" Suzy asked this question like she had some brilliant TV courtroom twist up her sleeve, but when she turned her back to everyone but Billy, she gave him an I-have-no-idea-what-I'm-doing face.

She's lost, thought Fame to Billy.

That's fine, thought Billy. *Tell her to keep going*.

"I don't understand the question," said a very confused adult.

Suzy whipped around with all of the confidence of a master attorney. "We, the students, need to be punished because we broke the rules. What rules would those be?"

"Well, to start—"

"Never mind," Suzy didn't want to go down that road. "We'll stipulate that rules were broken. What punishment are you proposing?"

"I think—"

She interrupted again. "Certainly, the punishment should fit the crime, otherwise, why are we bothering to learn all of this American History."

Suzy asked if this is making any sense, thought Fame.

Tell her it's brilliant!

"Certainly," said the befuddled federal board member.

"Of course, it should be said that the punishment should fit the rule-breaking, since I'm not sure we've actually broken any laws."

"I can think of a few broken laws," said the Fed.

"You really want to put these kids on trial?" asked Dillon.

Another federal board member whispered to the one who had been doing all the talking. The latter then spoke up but clearly wasn't happy about being forced into a corner by a 13-year-old and a principal who he had all but ignored up until then. "No, of course not."

"Good," said Suzy, "we're not going to jail. So the question is still, why do you feel the federal school board should have any say in the punishment for kids breaking local school rules?"

"If you would like," said Dillon, "I can have every kid caught chewing gum or running in the halls sent to your office for judgment."

The Fed clenched his jaw and looked around the room for support. When he found none, he said, "Fine. Punishment will be handled at the local level."

Dillon said, "As the student body president, Charles, do you agree to submit those students involved in this 'Kids In Power' sit-in to a punishment administered by me, which shall be appropriate for the breaking of rules?"

It was a loaded question. Dillon included the K.I.P. reference to let them know he was on their side. "Without admitting any guilt," said Charles, who clearly enjoyed the chance to almost practice law, "I can accept those terms."

"Any other questions my 13-year-old daughter can help you folks with?" asked a proud and exhausted Mrs. Quinofski. When there were none, she asked, "So we are all in agreement?"

Quiet nods meant the protest was over.

"Good," said Mrs. Quinofski. "Let's get these kids back to class."

Thirteen

School the Cops

"I REMEMBER YOU!"

Detectives Danner and Reins had that deer-in-the-headlights expression the kids learned to recognize from people who'd had their memories restored. General Quinofski must have refreshed them right before Suzy and Billy got back from school.

"You should," said Suzy to Detective Danner, who gawked at her with his finger loosely pointing in her direction, "you interrogated me for a whole day."

"I did?"

"Wait for it..." said Suzy.

The light bulb went off in Danner's memory. "I did!"

"There it is! Welcome back to the real world."

Detective Reins was still lost in a fog. "You went missing," he said to Suzy. "Did we ever find you?"

"No," said Suzy. "I'm still missing."

"Suzy," warned her father, "it's hard enough getting one's memory back without the sarcasm."

"Sorry, Dad."

"Snarky," said Danner. "I remember." He spoke as if his interview with Suzy had been decades ago, not the previous school year. Still, he gave her a wink.

"All right, gentlemen," said the General, "I wish we had time to shake more cobwebs loose, but we have a problem and need your assistance."

The General paused for a response, but the two officers just sat and strained their brains for a second. Finally, Reins had an a-ha moment. "The tape."

"Exactly," said the General.

"That professor guy… Too much cologne."

"Dr. Menaus," said Billy.

"We think he's the reason we all lost our memories," said Suzy. She put one leg up on the arm of the couch and sat like she thought a tough-chick TV cop would.

"Do we still have the tape?" asked Danner.

"We just watched it," said Reins.

"I mean, the tampered part of the tape. We could bring him in for that."

"No, you can't," said Billy. That earned him some, you-don't-know-what-you're-talking-about looks from the cops. Billy explained. "Don't you think you would have done that before? For all we know, we've had this conversation a hundred times and each time you go to arrest him, he wipes our memories again."

"Smart kid," said Reins to the General.

"Sci-fi 101," said Billy. "It's like a time loop, but with a memory twist, a no-brainer, really."

"All right then," said Danner, "What do you suggest we do?"

"That's easy," said Billy. "It's two wands against one."

"FOOLS RUSH IN WHERE wizards fear to tread."

General Quinofski paraphrased the old saying, but however he said it, it boiled down to the same thing for the kids. They would have to wait before taking any action.

"Why can't Billy zap Menaus's wand to bits?" asked Suzy.

"It may come to that," said her dad. "But as Billy said when you two first invented it, this is technology. If you destroy one, Menaus will make another."

"If I could figure out how he wiped our memories, I could do the same thing to him," said Billy.

"That's a thought, too," said the General, "but we have to consider the law." He asked Danner, "How do you think the courts would rule on memory wipes?"

"Unconstitutional for sure," said Danner. "Illegal search and seizure."

"But he did it to us," said Suzy.

"Yeah," said Reins, "but he's a bad guy. Bad guys don't have to play by the rules or care about others. They just do what's good for them. That's what makes them bad."

"We have to do something sooner than later," said Billy. "You heard the Teacher. They want a wand, and trust me, they are good at getting what they want."

The General twirled a rubber band around his index fingers. "What do you think the chances are they'll get his wand?"

Billy was ever the good scientist. He said, "Close to a hundred percent," while thinking 99.99999999 percent.

"There's an old war tactic," said the General. "If you know you're going to lose an asset, then turn it into a Trojan Horse. Can we make his weapon do what we want it to do, without Menaus knowing about it?"

"So Menaus will think the wand doesn't work," said Suzy.

"And if they get the wand?" asked her father.

"They won't be able to use it against us," answered Suzy.

Billy's head snapped up from a tired droop. "How do we do that?" He tried not to be as worn-out as he was, but apparently wasn't successful.

"That's a good question, Billy," said the General, "but tired brains are not going to come up with an answer. Why don't you kids take a break, while the cops and I work on the non-magical part of the plan."

Billy and Suzy didn't need Fame to translate their thoughts. No matter how much they argued, her dad wasn't going to back down. "Walk you home?" asked Suzy.

"Sure."

Fame joined them as soon as they stepped outside, which brought up a sore point with Suzy. "Why don't you tell dad about Fame? I mean, he's seen her a couple of times now."

As a person and a cat, but not both, thought the cat.

"I don't know," said Billy, "but the Teacher said to be paranoid."

Fame changed into her human form. "That's not exactly what he said."

"Should you be changing like that out in public?" asked Suzy.

"I've only changed in your heads," said Fame. "To everyone else, you two are talking to a cat."

"Any news on Dr. Cologne?" asked Suzy.

"He's been quiet. He does some magic in the evenings, but nothing big. He made a pile of old money appear in his living room and spent the rest of the night counting and stashing it in the vault he created in his magical house."

"Why old money?" asked Suzy.

"Why money at all?" asked Billy. "He's got magic. Who needs money?"

"Not very imaginative."

"I don't know," said Billy. "He imagined that memory spell. I still don't know how he did that, and we're going to need a defense against it when the time comes." The three of them walked in silence for a couple of steps before Billy asked, "Any ideas?"

Suzy started in on her favorite subject: brains. "In general, there are three types of memory: perception, short-term, and long-term. The first two are mostly electrical. Long-term memories, which is what Menaus was dealing with, aren't completely understood."

"Well, Menaus is a physicist," said Billy, "so his understanding of memory will probably be less than yours."

"Right. He'll probably know that memories are more like patterns in the brain. Nerve cells are connected by synapses where electrical impulses trigger chemical neurotransmitters that are received by dendrites. If I was going to attack someone's memory, that's where I'd do it, dendrites in the hypothalamus."

"I have no idea what you just said," said Fame.

Billy was quicker on the uptake. "What are dendrites?"

"They're like tree branches that reach into neighboring cells to help transmit electro-chemical connections between the cells. Memories — at least, what we know about them so far — are made... I don't know exactly how to explain it, but they are made by the way certain nerve cells are connected. The stronger the connection, the better the memory."

"Sort of like the way our thoughts reach out to connect us in the Quantum World," said Billy, thinking of how he followed family members' thoughts to find their lost loved ones.

"Yeah, I guess," said Suzy. "I suppose it's possible he imagined the connections that mean 'magic wand' in each person and broke part of that connection, but I don't know how he would do it."

"I do." Billy thought about his mother's electroshock therapy. "Electricity."

"So we have to protect our brains from electricity?"

"That's easy enough," said Billy. "The hard part is going to be how to make his wand do what we want."

"THIS IS A FIRST."

When Billy and Suzy walked into school the next day, the kids in the hall broke into spontaneous applause. "For you, maybe," said Billy.

"Oh, you've been applauded at school before?" asked Suzy.

"No, and I still haven't. This is for you."

As if on cue, some of the kids shouted, "Su-ZEE!"

In Biology, the old textbooks were handed out and Mr. Conner played the episode of PBS's Nova about the *Katzmiller v. Dover* court case on intelligent design. "Keep in mind," he told the class, "that this documentary is presented by a TV show on science. Still, I think it's a fair presentation of the evidence. When it's done, we'll discuss if you think intelligent design is worth teaching in a science class."

Mr. Conner sat down next to Suzy as the show began. "I've seen this," whispered Suzy.

"I figured you had. Would you like to study in the library?"

"No thanks. It's worth watching again."

"Knowledge is power," said Mr. Conner.

The discussion afterwards was heated, though only two kids supported the idea that intelligent design should be taught. Suzy asked if the Theory of Evolution would ever be declared a Law, like Gravity, but that started a whole political debate. Neither she nor Mr. Conner had any success explaining the difference between a "law" in science, and a "law" written by government.

As soon as the bell rang, Suzy realized she might want to skip her next class. It was study hall, where Billy was bound to talk to Linda about her relationship with Peter.

"THAT'S NONE OF your business."

Billy had zero experience talking to anyone about his or her love life, much less an edgy, gothic, high school senior. Suzy was shocked Linda didn't punch him in face.

"My brother is my business," said Billy.

"Leave it alone, Billy!" warned Linda.

"Or what?"

Suzy saw Billy's hand creep up his sleeve, where she knew he kept his wand, and got worried. "Billy…"

Linda's answer struck Billy harder than any spell would have. "Or you might learn more about life than you're ready for."

He said nothing, and his hand stopped moving.

"Your brother will be fine," said Linda. "Nothing could break his heart."

"I don't know about that." To everyone's surprise, that assessment came from Suzy. "He's grown up a lot in the last year."

"We all have," said Linda. "And not just last year. Last weekend was enough for me."

"Amen to that," said Suzy.

Even Billy's limited skills at reading social cues were good enough to notice the body language between Linda, her coven, and Suzy. Linda's silence about her weekend had put a wedge between her and her coven that Billy could see as clearly as if it were made of steel.

"I HEAR SOME EXTRA credit is in order."

History class with Ms. Fuller was something Billy, Suzy, and probably every other kid in the class would never forget. The discussion started with how they discovered Ms. Fuller's book in the library. That led to questions about her writing. What made her want to write? How many books had she written? And did she know J.K. Rowling? All the while, Ms. Fuller kept her gradebook open, handing out 'A's to anyone who could articulate what they did during the sit-in.

Suzy didn't say much, but she got an A anyway. Ms. Fuller had seen her speeches on TV, and told her has much. "You all probably learned more about American History during the protest than I could have taught you in years," said Ms. Fuller. "But now that it's over, work as usual will begin tomorrow."

Billy and Suzy didn't have to say it. It wasn't over for either one of them, not by a long shot.

Fourteen

GOOD V. EVIL

P AIN AND PRESSURE in Billy's chest woke him from a deep sleep. He found himself pinned to the bed by a wooden staff. It was held by a man he couldn't see in the dark of his bedroom. "They say it's your wand or mine, Billy, and it's not going to be mine!"

The smell of Dr. Menaus's cologne cleared the sleep from Billy's brain. His wand was under his pillow, but his hands were too far away to grab it without Menaus pushing his staff through Billy's chest.

"So do you hand it over peacefully, or do I rip you and this pathetic excuse for a home apart?"

Billy had to act fast. "At least my home is real," he said to buy some time.

The learned doctor's response was to jab Billy in the

stomach with his staff and roll him off the bed. "My bet is that it's under your pillow."

The stomach hit kept Billy from speaking, but he could still think. *Fame! Take my wand to Suzy right now!*

Before he got a response, Menaus tossed pillows to the floor.

Billy panicked but still had wits enough to think to Fame. *Tell Suzy she's going to have to reboot my memory in the morning.* His mind then started to work on how he might fight him once the professor had both wands.

Menaus searched the sheets. "Not here? You're not as smart as I thought." He grabbed Billy by the collar of his T-shirt, dragged him to his feet and slammed against the wall. "I'm going to ask you this once, Billy. If you don't answer, you're dead."

For a brief second of panic, Billy believed what he was told. Then he realized, "You can't kill me, Dr. Menaus. I'm the only one who knows where my wand is."

It wasn't hard for Billy to see thoughts flash behind Menaus's eyes, since they were just inches from his. Doubt and fear flared first, followed quickly by a steely resolve. "You have a brother, don't you? And a mother?"

Billy had only ever played one game of poker in his life, but he was quickly learning what it meant to bluff. "You won't hurt them," he said with more confidence than he had any right to. "You need me to be happy and healthy so I can be here to answer your questions about how the wands work." Billy quickly followed his double-speak with a question. "How many times have you talked to me before wiping my memory?"

Menaus tightened his grip. "Billy, if they take my

wand I won't have any reason to talk to you ever again."

"Really? I got my wand back from them. Hurt my family and you'll never find out how."

Before Menaus could respond, blue and white lights flashed around the room, followed closely by single blast from a police siren.

BILLY WOKE UP STANDING in his room, which was filled with the familiar lights of a police car in his front yard. "What has Peter done now?" he asked himself. On his way to the front door, he caught a big whiff of too much expensive cologne.

"Officer Carl," said Billy before he opened the door, "What's with the man-fume? Do you have a big date after work?"

"Billy, it's me."

He opened the door to find Suzy holding a stick in her hand, which flashed lights just like a police car. Curled around her feet was an uppity black cat. "When did you get a cat?"

GENERAL QUINOFSKI was in Washington, D.C., preparing for a Senate hearing, so Suzy's mom oversaw the restoration of Billy's memory. They showed him the breakfast video. His memories didn't take nearly as long to return as the other people who'd gone through it. "The patterns for magic in your brain are probably stronger than for the rest of us," said Suzy. "What happened to your 'that's easy' memory defense?"

Billy didn't make eye contact. He was still cleaning up the inside of his brain like it was an office hit by a hurricane. He did finally manage to say, "I was going to make a quantum Faraday cage, but I couldn't get to my wand."

"You mean like a tinfoil hat?" Suzy laughed, then stopped. She remembered what they had learned about schizophrenia. "I wonder if that's why paranoid people wear them."

"There's more." Billy's demeanor changed from intensely focused to relaxed and distant in a way that gave Suzy and her mom a sense of foreboding. "Dr. Menaus killed Dr. Parkson."

Billy explained that he now had new memories that hadn't returned before. Memories about Menaus making surprise visits to question Billy about how the wands work. When he told them the story of Dr. Parkson and the vintage car, Mrs. Quinofski called the police.

That was around one in the morning. It was nearly two-thirty by the time Billy had retold his story to detectives Danner and Reins. By four o'clock they had gotten off the phone with General Quinofski. They all agreed that Menaus was more of a threat than they had anticipated, but there was nothing they could do about the killing without having to present a magic wand in open court. That day would certainly come, but they weren't ready for it yet. They decided to boost their surveillance to 24/7. The General said he would loan the detectives some manpower in the form of Military Police.

That's about when Billy and Suzy lost interest in the conversation of police budgets, logistics, and military vs. civilian authorizations, blah, blah, blah. Billy had a better idea. *Fame*, he thought.

Their cat trotted into the room and curled up on Billy's lap. *I was wondering when you'd get around to thanking me.*

Absolutely, thought Billy. *Thank you.*

Just doing my job. I protect you two, and I protect your wands.

Suzy smiled at Billy. Obviously, Fame was thinking to both of them.

Billy got to his point. *Do we have any yard gnomes on our side?*

IT TAKES SOMETHING big to get Billy and Suzy to stay home from school. General Quinofski appearing live on all of the cable news channels during a Senate hearing qualified as big. That, and they didn't get to bed the night before until it was time to wake up the next day.

"He looks tired," said Suzy to her mom as they watched her father on TV.

He was in the middle of answering a question about what more could be done to stop lone-wolf terrorists in the military. "There is always an element of risk. How we mitigate that risk defines us as a nation."

Ed Cross, a senator from Texas that Billy had seen on the news from time-to-time, was asking the questions. "Do you think, General, it's too much to ask that our soldiers prove their loyalty to God and Country?"

"As to an individual soldier's loyalty to God," said General Quinofski, and he then quoted the opening clause of the First Amendment by heart, "'Congress shall make no law respecting an establishment of religion, or prohibiting the free exercise thereof.' If you're going to pass a law asking a U.S. citizen to swear an allegiance to God, that's fine, but it will have to be that individual's

God or gods and not one that Congress predetermines to be the correct one."

"Even if they worship witches?" The senator laughed at what he perceived to be the most ridiculous thing possible. No one joined him.

"I assume you're talking about my daughter," said the General.

"Oh, crap." Suzy wanted to hide. Not only was Billy there, having slept in the guest room for a few hours after last night's events, but so were her mom and some military friends who came over for a watch party/support group. The tension expanded to such a level that Billy feared it might break down the walls.

"If the shoe fits, General."

"I don't know what you mean by that, Senator, but I am happy to have the chance to read into the record how proud I am of my daughter and her classmates for exercising their rights to peaceably assemble, speak freely, and redress their grievances."

"You're even proud of her … what do they call themselves, 'Wiccan' friends?"

General Quinofski jumped on the condescending question without hesitation. "I'm proud of all U.S. citizens, Senator Cross. From first-generation newborns to gang bangers on death row, they are all the people living under the rules of the Constitution I swore to defend." He quickly corrected himself. "We *both* swore to defend. We don't get to pick and choose which Americans deserve Constitutional rights and which do not."

"What if her Wiccan friends had been Muslim?"

"There's no law against being Muslim, Senator."

"Maybe there ought to be." The senator said that not so loudly as to be an official statement, but not so quietly that the microphones couldn't pick it up. "That oath we took, General, says we must defend the Constitution against enemies both foreign *and* domestic."

"That it does, Senator. If *anyone* tries to deny an American their First Amendment rights, then that makes that person an enemy of the Constitution. That includes members of Congress."

The Texas senator leaned forward in his chair and pointed his finger at Quinofski. If it were a gun, he'd have pulled the trigger. "Are you questioning my loyalties, General?"

"Are you questioning mine?"

Cross backed down in words only. He knew there would be limited political gain in pressing a man with so many medals on his chest. "Certainly not."

"Why not?" General Quinofski didn't wait for an answer. "This hearing is to determine how we can test the loyalties of American soldiers. I'm an American soldier. I have put my life in the hands of the fighting men and women under me, and I will do it again and again and again without regard to a Good-American's Seal of Approval from the U.S. Congress."

"Then how do you propose we protect your fighting men and women from terrorists among their ranks? How do we sort out the Good from the Evil?"

General Quinofski took a deep breath and leaned back in his chair. "I've been giving that a lot of thought lately."

Billy whispered to Suzy as they watched, "Us, too."

"Seriously," she said.

Back in Washington, the General continued. "The enemy we face today is not a country. The battlefield is not on earth, but in our hearts and minds. Sure, we can close our minds to the enemy; we can build walls around our hearts. But military history tells us that fixed fortresses always fall. Like every war that has ever been fought, it cannot be fought the way the last one was.

"We face at least one generation of lost minds and hearts. Regretfully, there may only be a military solution for that generation, but if we are to win this war, we must find a way to reach out to their children, to win the battle for their hearts and minds ... even as we fight their parents.

"We're not going to win a war of Good versus Evil with a closed fist. We're not going to win this war by interrogating our own soldiers and spreading fear and mistrust among our ranks. Yes, our military needs to fight like Hercules, but our civilians need to fight like Gandhi."

The senator interrupted the silence that followed the General's speech. "And how are we supposed to do that, General? Wave a magic wand?"

Of the viewers who noticed the General's sideways glance into the camera or the nearly imperceptible Mona Lisa smile, few of them knew what it meant, and three where in the Quinofskis' living room.

"YOU'VE HAD AN eventful week."

Dr. Weston's point caught Billy off guard. "Has it only been a week since everyone got their memory back?"

If Dr. Weston had been a dog, her ears would have

popped up and pointed forward. "Excuse me?"

Uh-oh. Billy hadn't thought to ask General Quinofski if it was okay to talk to Dr. Weston about magic. "Oh… uh…" The wand and everything about it was Top Secret. "Nothing."

"No," said Dr. Weston. "You said something about everyone getting their memory back."

"Yeah… I can't talk about that."

"Why not?"

"It has to do with a top secret military operation," said Billy. "If I talk about it, I could get in a lot of trouble."

"Really?" Dr. Weston made a note on her pad in a way that made Billy realize how crazy he sounded. "Who would you get in trouble with?"

"I'd rather not say."

"Just the military in general?"

"A general has something to do with it," said Billy.

"What about the police?"

"Yeah, they're in on it, too."

"And the FBI?"

"No, not the FBI," said Billy, followed quickly by, "Can we change the subject?"

"I'd rather we didn't."

"I'd rather we did. Can I ask you a question?"

"Of course."

"We talked about Evil."

"Yes, we did." If Dr. Weston's ears perked up before, her whole body was in on it now.

Billy noticed how she leaned forward and focused on his every word. He figured he'd set off some kind of internal psychiatric alarm, but he couldn't worry about what she thought of him right at that moment.

"I need a real definition of Good and Evil."

"What do they mean to you?" she asked.

"What they mean to me isn't relevant." Billy tried to suppress the urgency in his voice, figuring that it wouldn't help his cause to sound crazier than he already did.

"I think it is."

"No, I need to be able to communicate this to…" How could he explain it? General Quinofski didn't want them to destroy Menaus's wand. Billy thought he might come up with a way that it couldn't be used for Evil. He wanted to limit the wand to only doing Good, but to do that, he had to know what Good and Evil were, exactly. Of course, he couldn't tell Dr. Weston that. The only reason he'd asked her was because the General was in Washington, and Billy figured if anyone should know what Good and Evil were, it would be a psychiatrist. Finally, he said, "I am trying to write a computer program that can only be used for Good."

"Oh." Dr. Weston relaxed a bit. "Is this part of the top secret project?"

"Uh…" Billy was having a hard time keeping up with what Dr. Weston must have thought was going on. "Sure."

That answer seemed to have put her more at ease. "Have you looked up 'Good' in the dictionary?"

"Yeah," said Billy. "All of the definitions depend on other words like 'morality' or 'benefits,' which are as hard to define."

She checked her watch, which Billy had learned over

the weeks meant it was almost time to go. "You've asked a good question, Billy. One that has boggled the minds of philosophers for centuries. This is the kind of thing you can think about for years, and have fun doing it. So, take your time, and it's not really top secret."

Great advice, except he didn't have time, and it was top secret.

"WOW, ZEE VITCHEZ' MINDS have gotten strawnger."

Winston High's favorite French exchange student was back.

"Do you have to keep the accent when no one else is around?" asked Suzy.

"Bettah zafe zan zorrEE."

Suzy had noticed, "the witches have been much less ... witchy this year. Why is that?"

"Zey had zomezing to fight against."

"I have no idea what you just said," said Billy.

She switched to thoughts. *Idle hands are the Devil's workshop.*

"The Devil?" asked Billy, "is he real?"

Don't be so literal.

"I think what she means," said Suzy, "is that the protest gave them something to focus on."

Exactly. Conflict makes a person's true colors shine. The good will become better, the bad, worse. Fame squinted in the Coven's direction. "I zee a problem between zem."

"They've been acting funny ever since we showed up in Linda's basement," said Suzy. "I think the other three know she's keeping a secret from them."

"Zecretz are not good."

"We're keeping a secret from the whole world," said Suzy.

Billy's attention stayed on the Coven. "You know… they might be able to help us." Without another word, Billy walked across the courtyard to the Coven's table. Suzy and Fame scurried to catch up.

"Hi," said Billy.

Three of the girls seemed to be equally annoyed and curious by Billy's intrusion on their lunch. Linda seemed nervous.

Billy didn't take notice of their body language. "I have a magic-related question."

Linda scowled. "I thought we weren't—"

Billy raised his hand and shook her off with a don't-worry-about-it gesture. "I've been wondering. If you're a good witch—"

"You mean a white witch?" asked Lisa Chang.

Billy didn't know what he meant, but Lisa mistook the confused look on his face. "No, that's not a racial thing. Laypeople think there are white witches and black witches, as in good and evil."

Mary took over. "In fact, there is white magic and black magic, and a witch can do either depending on her mood."

"We all have good days and bad," said Sonni.

Linda didn't join in the lesson of witchcraft delivered with the usual condescending tone. Instead, she asked, "What's your question?"

"Okay," said Billy. "Say you're a … witch who is predominantly into white magic and you want to stop a witch you who is mostly into black magic. How do you stop them from doing evil stuff?"

"That's easy," said Lisa.

"You bind them," said Mary.

"Magically, not with ropes or anything," corrected Sonni.

Their answers came with a flippant tone. Linda's did not. "You bind the witch to keep her from being a harm to herself or others."

"Who decides what is harmful?" asked Billy.

"Gaia," said Linda. "Mother Nature. The life force."

Billy nodded as he took in this information. "Thanks," he said as much for the answer as for taking his question seriously. "You wouldn't know how I could get in touch with her, would you?"

Fifteen

READY OR NOT

"**S**IR?" ASKED BILLY, "I think I have an idea how to turn Menaus's wand in our favor."

"I'm listening." General Quinofski had returned from Washington just after Suzy and Billy got home from school. Billy started up on the wand before the General could close the front door behind him.

"It sounds simple. I want to cast a spell on his wand so it can tell the difference between Good and Evil, and only do Good spells."

The General put down his suitcase, hugged Suzy, and focused in on the plan's central problem. "But whose definition of Good?"

"Yeah," said Billy. "I'm trying to come up with a scientific definition of Good and Evil, like an equation in a computer program. If I can get that, I think I can make the spell work."

"A lot of people get stuck on that," said the General.

"Everyone says that Goodness is in a person's heart, but that isn't really the case, is it? I mean, a heart just pumps blood."

"I can't define it, but I know it when I see it," said the General.

"What?"

"Nothing," he said quickly, and made his way to the kitchen. "That's what a Supreme Court Justice said about … something entirely different. Go on with what you were saying."

Suzy followed her father before Billy did, so she picked up the subject. "The Witches of Winston High told us about binding a bad witch so she can do no harm to herself or others, you know *Primum non nocere*."

Billy was right behind her. "I don't know if that'll work, since harm isn't defined."

"But you know in your heart what it means," said Suzy, "and the wands have always been good at, I don't know, filling in the blanks."

"Yeah, and that got Dr. Parkson killed," said Billy.

Both kids turned to the General, who had gotten into the kids' afterschool snack. He spread some peanut butter onto a cracker, then showed Billy what he was doing. "You have to make a little trench for the honey."

"He knows, Dad. I showed him that ages ago."

He filled the peanut butter trench with honey, put

another cracker on top, and popped the entire thing into his mouth. Suzy handed him her glass of milk, from which he took a big swig. "Thanks, Suz." He wiped his mouth with a paper towel. "I like the idea of all wands being bound by the Hippocratic Oath."

"Me, too," said Billy. Suzy nodded. So far their invention was responsible for two dead terrorists and Dr. Parkson. Granted, last year Billy had used it to prevent a nuclear war in Kashmir and saved a score of American soldiers, but he'd have preferred to have done that without harming anyone.

The General thought out loud. "I wish I could run this past our cyber-defense unit."

The kids didn't reply to his rhetorical comment. "Two questions," he said, then corrected himself. "No. One question, one concern."

Again, the kids didn't say anything.

"Question: Can we test it?"

Billy had thought of this as well. "Yes, with Suzy's wand."

"Concern…"

Billy knew what the concern was. He didn't like it, but he didn't have an argument against it, either.

"You're thirteen, Billy."

"Yes, sir." His tone revealed his low mood.

"I know you're smart. You're mature. I know you have a strong sense of Right and Wrong. I know this is important, more important than any of us can comprehend, but I'm not willing to put you at risk. Right now, you're one of our biggest assets."

Billy might not have had an argument, but Suzy did.

"But Dad, if we can bind Menaus's wand, then there won't be any risk. All we have to do is let them take it. The binding will do the rest."

"Sir," said Billy, "We were in danger the minute Suzy and I made a magic wand. This plan is the only hope we have of getting out of danger."

IT WAS LATE FOR a school night. Billy had stayed for dinner while he and the Quinofski family discussed Project Hippocratic Oath. They concluded that the kids would stay home from school the next day to test the Oath on Suzy's wand. If it worked, they would tell detectives Danner and Reins that they were ready to talk to Menaus.

You should walk Billy home. Fame's suggestion came after Suzy said she was too tired.

"Why?" asked Suzy out loud.

The Teacher wants to talk to both of you.

"On second thought," said Suzy to her parents, "I think I will walk Billy home."

Billy had heard Fame's side of the conversation, so he didn't ask questions. "Yeah, okay."

As soon as they closed the door behind them, Billy and Suzy were surrounded by the Teacher's voice, which boomed like a god's. "You understand that I'm a part of the collective consciousness?"

"Yeah, kind of, I guess," said Billy, "but I don't understand where you are right now."

"Sorry." His voice now came from between the two of them. There the Teacher, dressed like a cross between Obi-Wan Kenobi and a five-star general, walked casually with a perfectly normal voice.

Suzy worried about base security. "No one else can see you, right?"

"That depends on if they expect to see me."

Don't worry about it, thought Fame to both of the kids. *No one will see him.* Apparently, she wasn't so sure about herself, since she stayed in her cat form, trotting along between the three of them.

"Tell me how I exist," said the Teacher.

"As far as I know, you're a being of the collective consciousness," said Billy. "Meaning that so many people have an image of an old man with long white hair and a beard, who is the wise old wizard, or god, or whatever, that their thoughts keep you alive."

"*Alive* isn't exactly the right word, but yes. The collective human consciousness gives me great power."

"But…?" asked Suzy.

The Teacher gave a nod of respect to his latest pupil. "But mine is not the only image your kind obsesses over. In fact, I think you humans spend more time and energy on forms of my counterpart than you do me."

"What do you mean, 'counterpart'?" asked Billy. He felt like he knew the answer but was afraid to say it out loud.

"I mean demons, monsters, fiends, and an untold number of names for evil beings tied to nearly every religion or mythology on the planet."

Suzy checked to see if Billy was as scared by this conversation as she was. No one else would have noticed, but she could tell. His eyes flicked around. His hands twitched. His breathing was shallow. No doubt about it: Billy was scared.

"Every time one of you thinks about an evil being," said the Teacher, "no matter the context, the beast grows stronger."

"No matter the context?" asked Suzy, "You mean, when someone preaches *against*, say, Satan...?"

"They actually make him stronger," said the Teacher. "Fear is a powerful energy source to their kind. Fear and paranoia are the obvious foods for Evil, but there are so many others. The arrogance of righteousness. The spreading of ignorance. Hubris."

"So all of our thoughts about evil beings...?" asked Billy.

"Have created them," answered the Teacher. "They are known by many names, as am I. They are very powerful."

As are you, thought Fame, trying to rally her troops.

Billy swallowed hard as the realization of what they were up against sank in. He knew how powerful the Teacher was, and that he might not always be on their side. "So you're saying, sir, that beings like you exist, but they are Evil."

"Unspeakably so. Or, if you prefer, they have a profound lack of Goodness. Yin and Yang."

"So what should we do about them?" asked Suzy, but just that quickly, Billy and Suzy walked alone toward his trailer park home. "I keep forgetting not to ask him that question."

"ARE YOU READY?"

Billy and the Quinofski family gathered in Suzy's basement biology lab to test what had been dubbed Project Hippocratic Oath.

"What do I have to do?" asked Mrs. Q.

"Hopefully nothing," said Billy.

"So I'll sit here and think good thoughts," she said.

"For this first test," said the General, "yes."

Billy put out his hand. "Suzy? Your wand, please."

"I'll hang onto it. You won't get to take it from Menaus when we do this for real."

"Fair enough." Billy pointed his wand, said "*Primum non nocere*," and fired. A small spark popped from the tip, wrapped itself around Suzy's wand and disappeared as if it absorbed into it. "Did you feel anything?" he asked Suzy.

"No, nothing."

"Okay," said the General. "Try the first spell."

Suzy had done some easy Tap-Magic, as Billy called it, before the test as a control. She would try the same spells now to see if they worked. She pointed her wand toward a counter, said, "Treats!" and flicked the button. A white flash of energy leapt across the room, landed on the counter, and transformed itself into a plateful of...

"Oooh, cupcakes!" said Mrs. Quinofski when she saw what it was.

"But Mom, cupcakes are bad for you."

"Not always," said her mother. "Not in moderation."

"Okay, good," said her dad. "That was a slightly complex test of harm. Let's do the second one." He indicated some wrestling pads laid out on the basement floor. "Honey, if you'll step over here."

"Okay," she said. "This reminds me of basic training." To her daughter, she said, "Don't be afraid to punch hard, Mommy can take it."

"Dad, why aren't you doing this? Or Billy?"

"Because I won't let them," answered Mrs. Q. "I'm not sitting on the sidelines anymore. Come on, honey, punch my lights out." She took a boxer's stance and bounced on her feet.

Suzy took a position opposite her, but more like a fencer with her wand as the sword. "Okay, here it goes. PUNCH!" She flicked her wand.

Nothing happened.

"Try it again," said the General.

"Punch!" said Suzy. Again, nothing happened.

Without giving up her boxer's moves, Mrs. Quinofski waved Billy over. "Billy, try it with your wand."

Billy took Suzy's place. "Sorry, Mrs. Q."

"It's okay, Billy, I can take a punch in the name of science and saving the world."

"All right, here we go." He pointed his wand. "*Pugno percutio*," and fired.

A bolt of energy slammed into her chest, and down went Mrs. Quinofski. She hit the mat like sack of potatoes.

Suzy screamed and went to help her mother, followed by the men in the room.

Mrs. Quinofski stumbled to her feet, took a deep breath, which seemed to calm her down, and asked, "So, it worked then?"

"Seems to have, yes," said Billy.

"I'd like to do more tests," said the General. "Ratchet up the stakes if we can."

"I'm sure you would," said his wife in a way that made the kids think she wasn't too keen on the idea.

Out of nowhere, Fame, in cat form, leapt onto the couch. She arched her back and growled in that way real cats do in the face of trouble. With her thoughts, she shouted to the kids. *We've got to move. Now!*

"Fame!" said Billy, "What are you talking about?"

The Quinofskis all looked at Billy like he was crazy for talking to a cat, though Suzy just thought he was crazy for talking to a cat out loud. "Billy!?" she said.

"Oh, who am I kidding?" said Billy. "Fame? Can you take human form?"

"Sure thing," said Fame. She transformed into her tomboy façade, "but this better be fast."

General and Mrs. Quinofski jumped five feet in shock from the sudden visitor.

"General, Mrs. Q.," said Billy. "You've met Fame as a human before, but what you don't know is…"

"Isn't that your cat's name?" asked Mrs. Quinofski.

"Meow," said Fame.

The General smiled at the confirmation of his suspicions.

Billy got back to business. "Tell them what you told us."

"We have to move. The Teacher is running interference, but they are coming for Menaus's wand."

"We're ready," said Billy.

"We are?" asked Suzy and her mother at the same time.

"Sounds like we don't have a choice," said the General.

"That's right, sir," said Fame. "If they get the Menaus wand, we won't be able to protect it in our world. All hell will break loose. Literally."

"Billy, can you bind his wand from here?" asked Suzy.

"I don't know. It would be better to have a visual confirmation."

"Agreed," said the General.

"Dad. Billy can take point. I'll hang back in the quantum world and cover him."

The General grimaced and twisted around for a second like he wanted to dodge having to make this decision, but in the end he had no choice. "All right. Go, but you bind his wand and come right back, hear me?"

"Yes, sir," said the kids.

"Fame," said Suzy, "stay here and be our line of communication."

"Roger that," said Fame.

Billy saluted Suzy with his wand. "Ready?"

Suzy saluted back. "Ready."

"I'll drive," said Billy.

"Roger that," said Suzy. *Fame, count to three.*

One... two... three!

Together, the kids snapped their wands to their sides and disappeared with a flash of light and a low roll of thunder.

"WHERE ARE WE?"

Suzy couldn't see anything, but she heard Billy reply. "Still at your house — but, you know, the Quantum version. Open your eyes."

"I didn't close my eyes, why do I always have to keep opening them?"

"I don't know, but I always have to think my eyes open."

"Maybe it's a metaphor. 'There are none so blind as those who will not see.'"

"I like the second half of that saying, too," said Fame — who was not there. "'The most deluded people are those who choose to ignore what they already know.'"

"So much for a sound check," said Billy. "Follow me."

"How?"

"I don't know, just think about following me."

Billy thought of Dr. Menaus and began to fly off with Suzy right behind.

They flew through walls, over trees, around houses and other buildings. "It's like our dream!" said Suzy.

"Yeah, but this time it's real!"

Billy didn't actually know where he was going. He had been working in the lab at Oakridge Academy for as long as he could remember, so he had a strong connection with Dr. Menaus before this mess had started. He followed that connection to find Menaus's house.

"So, would this be considered a 'Man Cave'?" Suzy asked.

They were inside Dr. Menaus's house — in a Quantum sort of way. Billy had cranked up the reality dial enough for them to make out more details, but not so much that they would be detectable. On the other end of the scale, he had to be careful not to turn every particle of reality into what they had been or would be from the beginning to the end of Time. It was a delicate balance that Billy was close to perfecting.

"Find his wand and let's get out of here."

Billy had thought they would search the house in a conventional manner, but then remembered where he was. "Show me the magic," he whispered to himself.

Sure enough, everything in the universe disappeared except for a five-foot wooden staff a short distance away, which glowed with a red light.

"Nice," said Suzy.

With his finger still on the button of his wand, Billy said, "*Primum non nocere,*" and flicked it at Menaus's staff. A spark of energy fired from the tip of his wand, but dissipated before making it to the staff.

Suzy's gut churned with fear as something dark flew past her toward Billy. "Billy look out!" She fired her wand toward the dark mass, but nothing happened.

Billy turned and fired. "*Pugno percutio!*" The dark mass knocked backwards, then headed toward Suzy.

"Billy! I can't fight. Unbind my wand!"

Billy shot a magic bolt toward Suzy with his best take-it-back spell, "Oops."

"Thanks," said Suzy as she pointed her wand toward the dark mass. "*Scutum absconditum.*" Instead of her being surrounded by an invisible force field, her version imprisoned her attacker in an impenetrable ball.

"Nice variation," said Billy.

"Thanks. Now bind his wand and let's go home."

"Okay, I have to drop back into our world."

"Fine, just do it."

Billy didn't hear Suzy's impatient tone very often, so when he did he knew she was in no mood for discussions. He let go of the button.

As soon as Billy felt the floor underneath his feet, he was knocked down to it by Menaus who charged him from behind.

Billy didn't miss a beat. He pointed at Menaus's staff

just before the professor grabbed it and shot. *"Primum non nocere."* This time the magic found its mark.

Menaus didn't seem to notice, as he grabbed his staff and fired on Billy. "Die!"

Nothing happened.

Billy got to his feet. "You should do your spells in Latin. It sounds a lot cooler."

Menaus gave up on magic and charged Billy, using his staff as a more primitive weapon.

Billy shot again. *"Pugno percutio!"* Menaus took the full brunt of the magic punch, which slammed his back against the wall behind him. "See what I mean? Latin is cool."

From Menaus's gasps, Billy knew he'd had the breath knocked out of him so he wouldn't have a snappy response.

Billy sauntered toward Menaus. "They've run out of patience, Doc. They're coming for your wand, but before they do I have one question."

Menaus got his breath back. "Is it about the restraining order I'm going to have to get against you?"

Billy, Suzy says not to get too close, thought Fame. *She says he can still disarm you.*

Billy stopped his advance. Instead, he casually sat on the arm of a couch.

"How many times have we done this?"

Menaus smiled. "You mean the memory thing?"

"Yeah. The 'memory thing'."

"Well, if you count the first one — which didn't seem to take with you for some reason — there was your visit to Oakridge, and I dropped by your place for two or three little chats."

"Thanks. That would have bugged me if I didn't know."

"It's funny," said Menaus. He used his staff to help get to his feet, obviously still in pain. "Here I have the most powerful, world-changing, invention ever created and I can't talk to anyone about it."

"Maybe because you didn't invent it," said one of the true inventors.

"Yeah, well, that technicality can be managed. The real problem is, if I tell the world about magic, then it's no longer magical, is it? It's just technology."

"I think if you tell the world about magic then it would be criminal."

Menaus smiled. "You see, Billy, this is good. This is a good thing we're doing. Talking, I mean. I've really enjoyed our talks."

"Why don't you talk to the principal at Oakridge, and the police? You can tell them that you attacked me, instead of the other way around."

"Billy, we hold in our hands the power of God and I have no idea what to do with it. Do you?"

"I can think of a few things you can do with yours."

Menaus readied his staff and found his balance. "I guess we're beyond the memory tricks, huh Billy?"

Billy spread his hands wide, palms up, in an inviting gesture. "Give it your best shot."

Menaus hesitated for a moment. Billy noticed that he stole a quick glance at his staff to see if it might have been tampered with. Then, quick as lightning, with an evil scowl on his face, Menaus fired his wand at Billy.

Nothing happened.

"Have you checked the battery?" asked Billy. "That happened to me once. It's very embarrassing."

Billy, Suzy says more of those dark forms are gathering.

What are they doing?

She says they are just watching.

"The battery is fine." Obviously, Menaus knew nothing about what was happening in the Quantum World. That gave Billy an idea.

"Maybe you're not holding the button down long enough. Sometimes it takes a while to build up a charge."

Menaus fired his wand again. Again, nothing happened.

Fame, tell Suzy to get ready for a visitor.

She says she's way ahead of you.

To Menaus, Billy said, "No, I'm serious. It's not like you're going to be able to hurt me. I have a magic wand and a few tricks up my sleeve, so give it a good long blast."

Sure enough, Menaus fired his wand again. This time he held the button long enough to disappear into the Quantum Realm.

Sixteen

CLOSING THE DEAL

"T HERE YOU ARE."

Suzy's announcement came out as if she'd found a lost puppy. That thought turned Menaus into a cuddly little four-month-old German shepherd, which barked profusely.

"You have to learn to speak with your mind," said Suzy. "Things don't work around here the way you think they should."

"Actually," said Billy, who appeared right next to Menaus. "Things work around here exactly the way you think they should, which can make for some interesting scenarios."

"Billy? 'Scenarios'?" asked Suzy, "What have I told you about matching your vocabulary to your social surroundings?"

"So... 'sit, roll over, and beg' would be better?"

Suzy's laugh made the entire Quantum World fluffy, non-stick, cotton candy. "Totally!" Then she noticed that Dr. Menaus, as a man or a dog, was nowhere to be seen. "Where did he go?"

"He's still here. I can sense him."

"You mean smell him," said Suzy.

Suddenly, a pulse of red light flashed from a central spot in this ever-changing world. Behind it ran a roll of thunder.

"That's fear," said Billy. "Your fear, Dr. Menaus." This being the Quantum World, Billy did and didn't know where Menaus was, so he just spoke into space. "You see, your thoughts and emotions create electricity, and around here that energy defines reality."

A dry, harsh, quantum wind swirled quantum particles around like sand.

"I know this," said Billy, "Because I lived through it. And the thing is... How do I explain this? Ah... it gets worse."

Red lightning flashed across the universe. Sharp, piercing thunder cracked, nearly drowning out the screams of Dr. Menaus. "How do I get out of here?"

Of the three humans in the Quantum World, Billy had the most experience. He had been through a quantum panic attack, so he knew what to expect. Mentally, he reached out to find Suzy's hand and held it. If they were going to survive this, they would need each other's support.

Billy forced his voice to remain cool. "Getting out of this is easy. Just let go of the button on your wand."

Dr. Menaus sounded like he was in tears. "I don't know how." Menaus's cries sounded like the pathetic whimpers of a puppy frightened by a thunderstorm. The difference was, the quantum storm was much more dangerous.

Billy raised his wand, which wasn't entirely necessary since they were already in a world where thought created reality. He needed the gesture to focus his thought, which was calm. A bubble of stillness engulfed him and Suzy as a raging red sandstorm engulfed the rest of time and space.

"Come on, Doc," said Suzy. "You've got a Ph.D. in quantum mechanics. You should be able to figure out how to lift your finger."

Outside their calm realm, hell swirled. Then a deep, resonant voice drowned out the chaos. "Billy, Suzy, I hope you know what you're doing." It was the Teacher, and the kids couldn't tell from his voice if he was on their side or not.

Like the last time they were together in this crazy place, they saw giant fingers of black smoke rise in the distance and snake toward what had to be Dr. Menaus.

"No death!" shouted Billy. He whipped his wand toward the clouds of mortality, not sure how he would stop them. His subconscious, on the other hand, knew of a trick that nothing could overcome. Absolute Zero. Zero degrees Kelvin. The temperature at which every movement, even the vibration of molecules and the flight of electrons, stopped cold. Literally.

From the tip of his wand, a white stream that represented an absence of everything, shot toward Dr. Menaus, who materialized out of billions of particles that rushed in from everywhere. Billy's cold spell surrounded Menaus in a sphere of protection. When the black smoke touched the Absolute Zero shield, it froze, then vanished. The fingers that had yet to reach the doctor, retreated.

Suzy cheered. "Nice job, Billy!"

As she said that, the white shield dropped away. For a brief moment, there was calm. Then out of nowhere a giant tail lashed out toward Menaus. His scream cut short and all was silent.

Billy called out. "Dr. Menaus?"

Then Suzy. "Are you there?" When there was no response, she asked Billy, "Is he dead?"

"No," said Billy. "He's back in the human world. They got his wand."

FLAMES BURST AROUND the universe, and a red hand as large as a galaxy thrust Menaus' staff, which stretched from one end of infinity to the other, toward the kids. "Why won't this work?" asked a voice so deep and dark that it shook all of reality.

Billy froze.

"Billy!" shouted Suzy.

The deep voice spoke again. "'First do no harm?'" A head large enough to match a hand as big as a galaxy thrust into the light from the darkness of infinity and laughed in Billy's face. "Excellent."

Billy recognized the face; blood-red skin, sharp white teeth, long black hair with a thin goatee, and eyes that glowed a fiery gold. It was Satan. With Billy's realization, the beast roared in anger.

"Billy, is that who I think it is?" asked Suzy. Clearly, she saw the same face he did.

Her question brought Billy's focus back from emotion into logic. "No," he said. "Well, yes, he's the collective image of the Lord of the Underworld, but he's just a Quantum being like any other."

"Well, the other ones have pretty much proven they can kick our butts, so what are we going to do?"

"You're going to do nothing!" The Evil One backhanded Suzy, swatting her away like a fly.

"Suzy!" But Billy couldn't move. The Evil One held him like King Kong clutching Fay Wray.

"I don't need the wand to do harm. I can do all the harm I want by myself. I need the wand to do something as harmless as open a gate." He opened his hand, leaving Billy standing on his palm. "And, this is the important part, the wand must do nothing to stop me. Thanks, Billy. You've done exactly what I expected. Just like your brother. Just like your father. There's no such thing as a virtuous Bobble."

"Billy, what's he saying?" asked Suzy, who was now just a speck on the horizon.

"Why should you care about being good?" asked Satan. "Your father didn't care enough to stick around, so why should anyone else?"

And just like that, the Evil Beast was gone.

Standing next to Billy now, was a sharp-dressed man in a sharp-dressed suit. He put one hand on Billy's shoulder, and offered his other to shake. His voice was smooth and comforting. "Billy, do you know what great things I'm going to do with your invention?"

Billy didn't answer.

"No? I think you do. Do you know why I think you do?"

Again no answer.

"Because you and I, together, can do whatever you like. You want to solve the global warming problem? Wave your wand. You want to feed the hungry? Press the button and make it so. You want to cure your mother? We can do that together."

Suzy thought her way back into Billy's vicinity. "Billy, don't listen to him!"

The slickly dressed man waved his hand and Suzy disappeared. "The world has so many problems, Billy. Problems that we can solve with one little agreement."

Billy's head was spinning. After such a long time, someone was finally talking about doing the kinds of things with magic that Billy had been dreaming of. Sure, Billy didn't know what his intentions were, but hadn't the Teacher said there was a touch of Good in everything Evil, and the other way around? If Billy could be that touch of Goodness, what did the rest matter?

Finally, Billy spoke. "What agreement is that?"

"Simple," said the man, who had a rugged hand-someness that Billy couldn't help but admire. "I don't interfere with your magic, and you don't interfere with mine."

"Billy!" Suzy was shouting, but Billy couldn't tell where she was. Somewhere far away, so what could it matter?

"All I need you to do, Billy, is nothing. Just like Dr. Menaus's wand. Do no harm to me, or anyone for that matter." Once again, the man raised his hand for Billy to shake. "Deal?"

"Billy. Snap out of it."

Suzy was back and she was angry.

"Go away, little girl," said the man. "Men are doing business here. Billy, just shake my hand and we'll solve all the problems of the world."

"No!" said Suzy. She pushed the man with all of her physical and mental might. "Get out!"

It worked. The sharp-dressed man flew out of the picture like a cartoon character.

"Billy, you were about to make a deal with the Devil, literally."

"No, Suzy. He was going to help me do good things. I was going to save the world."

"At what cost?"

"Does it matter?"

"Yes! Billy, it matters very much."

Suzy. It was the Teacher's voice. *You don't have much time. Make him see.*

"See what?"

The lessons we've been teaching.

Suzy was in a panic? What lessons? She would have asked, but she sensed he was gone, and the evil guy was sure to be back any second.

When did the Teacher teach them lessons?

The realization hit her like a lightning bolt. Literally, sparks flew from her head. "Billy, in your dreams, what did Evil say to you?"

"He said he was Evil," said Billy as if it meant nothing.

"What else?"

"He asked me to join him."

"And did you?"

"No, of course not. He just told me he was Evil. Why would anyone knowingly team up with Evil?"

"Are you getting it now?" Suzy could feel the realization radiate from Billy like the heat of a rising sun.

A split second later, a mountain range rose up from nothing, separating Billy and Suzy.

Suzy shouted. "Fly, Billy!"

They both did, and met at the top of the highest mountain, where it became a beautiful, calm meadow. *Hurry, children*, thought the Teacher, *I can't hold him off forever.*

"Billy, what else did Evil say in your dreams?"

"He said he was cold."

"Billy! I completely forgot. Our second riddle, 'How can Evil be cold?'"

"That's not a riddle," said Billy. "There's no such thing as cold."

Suzy was flummoxed. "What?"

"In physics, cold is really a lack of heat," said Billy. "Ice has less heat than water, but more heat than frozen nitrogen."

"Billy! This is not the time for a physics lesson! We're in serious trouble here."

Billy looked at all the life in the meadow the Teacher had created for them. "What did you tell me about the men that discovered the structure of DNA?"

"Rosalind Franklin worked on it, too, but Billy snap out of it! We have to do something."

"Yes, we have to do something beautiful, Suzy. That's what you told me they said about DNA. They knew they had it right when it was beautiful, because when science uncovers the truth, there is a beauty in it. $E=mc^2$! The double-helix of DNA!" Billy was shouting with excitement. "The laws of thermodynamics!"

Suzy had to shout to keep up with him. "Billy! What are you talking about?"

Billy was more excited than Suzy had ever seen him. "Evil is cold. But Cold doesn't exist. Cold is just a lack of heat. And heat is really energy. It's movement. It's vibration on the molecular level. It's almost like life."

CRACK! Literally, a giant crack formed in the perfect blue sky of their quantum meadow. Black smoke poured in from the void beyond. Suzy knew what that meant. "Billy, hurry! Get to the point!"

Billy summed up to himself as fast as he could. He was so close to figuring out something fantastic. "Evil is Cold. But Cold doesn't exist."

"You said that before."

"So Evil doesn't exist. Cold is a lack of Heat. Heat is Goodness. So Evil is a lack of Goodness, you know, relatively speaking."

Suzy watched as the smoky fingers of death searched the meadow for the kids. "I don't care about relatively speaking, Billy. We need literally doing."

Billy's eyes popped with another a-ha moment. "That's it! That's why Evil didn't fight us from doing the Hippocratic Oath. He was even waiting for us to do it!"

"Billy!"

"What did the introduction to Mrs. Fuller's book say?"

"What?"

"The quote?"

"Edmund Burke, 'The only thing necessary for the triumph of evil is for good men to do nothing.'"

"What happened in our dream when you quoted the Hippocratic Oath?"

"The surgeon," Suzy quickly corrected herself, "the Teacher didn't operate, because cutting would harm the patient."

"We need to re-bind the wand, using the Laws of Thermodynamics."

They were out of time. The black smoke of death was about to engulf both of them. Suzy screamed, "Billy!" as she lost sight of her best friend.

BILLY WATCHED THE SMOKE block out his vision like a black fog. But when he spoke it was as if he and Suzy were on a leisurely walk home from school. "Take, for example, the Third Law of Thermodynamics." He fired his wand. A jet of complete absence of energy engulfed the smoke, which turned into a glass-like state, shattered, and disappeared.

"Finally!" said Suzy, who stood in the quantum void right next to him.

"The entropy of a system approaches a constant

value as the temperature approaches absolute zero," said Billy, quoting the law he just used to save them.

"Where are we?" asked Suzy. The Quantum World was completely without form or function.

"We're the same place we've always been, everywhere and nowhere all at once."

"Can we just re-bind Menaus's wand and get out of here?"

"Sure," said Billy. "Think about where his wand is so we can find it."

Instantly, the staff spun past them toward Earth, wherever that was. Behind it, a tornado of cold evil dragged Billy and Suzy toward their planet below.

Their destination lay ahead, the calm in the eye of the storm. There Billy saw green grass and Dr. Menaus twisting in agony.

Suzy saw it, too. She also noticed a large, dark mass shoot past her. "What was that?" she shouted. "I think it's alive!"

Billy shouted back, "Hang on." He pointed his wand toward the grassy spot and thought of a giant airbag.

Two additional dark, living, masses jetted past them before they spun through the whole. Billy and Suzy landed hard onto the soft airbag. Above them Menaus's staff held open a hole between the two dimensions, with more black-shrouded creatures flying out of it to all points of the globe.

"What's happening?" asked Suzy.

"I'd guess that those things are demons. They are escaping into our world."

"How do we stop them?"

Billy pointed his wand toward Menaus's staff, which spun like a fan, sucking evil beings from the Quantum World into the human one. "Exothermic only," he shouted as he fired at the hole between the two worlds.

The energy from his wand absorbed into the staff, which stopped spinning and sucked up into the Quantum World. The hole closed. The storm cleared.

"That's how we stop them," said Billy.

"DR. MENAUS, YOU'RE UNDER ARREST for obstruction of justice, tampering with evidence, and I don't know what else." Danner wasn't sure what he could charge Menaus with, without breaking the Top Secret military status. He and Reins had barged into the house when they heard fighting, only to find Menaus behind them lying face down in his front yard. That was followed shortly by the sudden appearance of an airbag, which caught Billy and Suzy falling from the sky.

While Danner put cuffs on Menaus, Billy came up with another charge. "How about practicing magic without a license."

"Is that illegal?" asked Reins.

"Not yet," said his partner, "but it might be soon." He winked at Billy.

"Attempted murder is another one," said Billy.

"Who did he try to kill?" asked Reins.

"Me." Billy's matter-of-fact tone made the officers do a double take. Billy ignored them.

"And don't forget Dr. Parkson," said Suzy.

"Yeah," said Billy, "tack on a murder charge."

"This is going to be an interesting case," said Reins as he and Danner took Menaus away.

"Suzy, we should get back to your place."

Suzy hadn't moved from where she landed on the extremely comfortable airbag. "You drive. I'm exhausted."

Seventeen

DEMON HUNTERS

H UGS AND CHEERS and kisses greeted Billy and Suzy on their return home.

"You're safe!" cried Mrs. Quinofski.

"It wasn't that big of a deal," said Suzy.

"Are you kidding? Your friend Fame gave us a blow-by-blow. I was scared to death!"

After a big group hug, General Quinofski shook Billy's hand. "Nice job, soldier."

"Thanks, sir."

After dropping Billy's hand, the General snapped a sharp salute.

Billy blushed. He wasn't sure how to respond to such high praise.

"Don't leave me hangin'," said the General.

Billy returned the salute. The General smiled and gave the boy a big hug. "How does it feel to save the world?"

"I'm not sure we did."

The Teacher appeared in the room. He wore a tuxedo that looked like something from the 1920s and carried a bottle of Champagne with glasses for all. "You're right," he said in response to Billy's comment. "You didn't save one world, you saved two — yours and ours."

Suzy shared Billy's doubt. "But sir, they got the wand."

"Yes, isn't that marvelous?" He and Fame laughed as Fame accepted a glass.

It was Billy's turn to question him. "It seems like a lot of his kind flew out of the hole he created."

The Teacher dismissed this with a gesture as if he were shooing a fly with his magnum of wine. "A handful. They'll have to be tracked down and dealt with, of course. But Billy, you and Suzy averted a new Dark Age, for sure."

"Really?" asked Suzy, with a spark of pride in her voice.

"I don't even know how you did it," said the Teacher. Not knowing seemed to put him a cheerful mood.

"But they still have Menaus' staff," said Billy.

"Yes, and they can't get it to work!" The Teacher was as giddy as a schoolboy. "My world is a mass of frustration from their side and laughter from ours. Billy, you are a genius!" He handed him a glass.

Billy took it. "I don't know. Without Suzy, I'm an idiot."

"Actually, sir, you're the one who taught us all of those lessons," she said.

The Teacher handed Suzy a glass, which she took after a "why not?" look of semi-approval from her parents. "I gave you the tools," said the Teacher. "You two created a solution I never would have thought of."

Billy and Suzy shared a look, then a blush, then they busted out in the face-hurting grins.

Mrs. Quinofski asked, "What exactly was that solution?"

"Yeah, Billy," said Suzy. "I know it's got something to do with exothermic reactions, but I don't get the rest."

Billy tried not to bust with pride over his idea. He wasn't entirely successful. "It was something Detective Reins said about bad guys only doing stuff that's good for them. In my dreams, Evil said…" Billy stopped himself, cocked his head to the side, then pointed to the Teacher. "That was you in my dreams, pretending to be Evil."

"Really?" said Suzy. "You're just figuring that out?"

The Teacher was more forgiving. "Yes, Billy. That's a role I play too well sometimes."

Billy got back on track. "Anyway… You said that Evil is like cold, meaning that it doesn't exist. It's just a relative lack of Good. That means Good is like heat, which is energy. So… an Evil spell would be one that sucked energy from the surroundings, which would make it cold, a.k.a. endothermic."

Suzy face-planted into her palm, "Billy, no one says

'a.k.a.'" She turned to her mother. "What am I going to do with him?"

From her smile, Suzy got the feeling she didn't want to hear the answer.

"I just said 'a.k.a.,' Suzy, and I am someone, so get over it." He stuck his tongue out at his friend and they both smiled. Billy got back to his explanation. "So what I did was bind the wand into only doing exothermic spells. That would be spells that add energy to the sur-roundings."

General Quinofski said, "In other words, you came up with an equation that defines the greater good."

"Exactly," said Billy. "The wand doesn't have to make a philosophical judgment. It just has to solve for entropy. Negative entropy means it's an exothermic spell, there-fore it is good. A positive total entropy would be evil. So, my spell was 'exothermic only.'"

"You kind of lost me on that last bit," said Mrs. Quinofski, "but as long as it works."

"Oh, it works." The Teacher raised his glass. "To young Master Bobble and Mademoiselle Quinofski, saviors of worlds."

Everyone answered the toast with a "here-here." Then Billy and Suzy got their first taste of Champagne, not realizing that the Teacher had removed the alcohol from their glasses.

The moment of celebration didn't last long. As casually as he could, General Quinofski brought up the bad news. "About these demons that got out."

The Teacher nodded. "Yes, General, I imagine you and those in your business are going to be busy for some time."

"I'm sorry to hear that," said the General.

The Teacher put his hands on Billy and Suzy's shoulders. "Keep these two close, and maybe it won't be as bad as it has been in the past."

"That is a cause for hope, sir," said General Quinofski, but by that time the Teacher had disappeared. "Does he always do that?"

"Pretty much." Billy smiled.

Suzy did too, for a second. Then her lips snapped back to seriousness. Then a smile again. She wasn't sure how to feel as the tension of last few days — and the intensity of the most recent fight — took over her body.

Mrs. Quinofski noticed Suzy's quivering chin. "It's okay, baby, let it go." She spread her arms.

Suzy dove into those arms. "Oh, Mom!" Tears of relief flowed like rain.

Billy shifted his weight, but he wasn't left hanging for long. Mrs. Q waved him over. "Billy, come on. Bring it in, and let it out."

As badly as he wanted to give into the child-side of his thirteen years, Billy hesitated in front of the General.

"Go on, son. You've earned a good cry. Every good soldier does it eventually."

For the first time in as long as he could remember, Billy let his guard down. He busted out in sobs and joined Suzy in her mother's embrace. Every tear took away a bucket of stress, and made room for the strength he would need to carry on.

General Quinofski joined the hug, but would later claim that he didn't cry. Colonel Quinofski would say that her husband was a liar.

"ONE THING I don't understand."

Billy's comment came while walking home with Suzy and Fame.

"What's that?" asked Fame.

"The Winston High Witches cast a spell to make me fail a test, and you showed up. Did they actually do magic?"

"I don't know about magic, but they got in touch, yes."

Suzy was as shocked as Billy. "Really?"

"How is that possible?" asked Billy.

"In many ways, it's sort of the way people like your mother can see into our world."

"You mean schizophrenics," said Suzy.

"Yes," said Fame. "That, and having your wand on our side of the barrier between our worlds weakened that barrier, sort of. It made it easier for thoughts to move from your side to ours. Evil took full advantage of this as soon as your wand crossed over."

"I didn't know that was possible," said Billy.

"It's happened before," said Fame. "In the Dark Ages, for example. So many people believed in witches, demons, etc., that our powers grew. Well, mostly the powers of those on the evil side of the spectrum."

"Your world is weird," said Suzy.

"We think the same thing about yours." Everyone smiled. "Especially when one of you conjure us up to do some crazy spell or something."

"So…" Billy couldn't believe he was asking this

question. "Magic works? I mean, witches, spells, potions, and stuff?"

Fame was quiet for a few steps, then said, "In science, do you ever say something is one hundred present true or false?"

"Rarely," said Billy. "There is always a chance for an anomaly."

"There you go," said Fame. "Traditional magic, witches and spells and potions and stuff, is ninety-nine point nine-nine-nine percent ineffective. At least where we Quantum folk are concerned. I don't know about self-fulfilling prophesies or the power of positive thinking, or anything like that."

The trio walked in silence up to the point where Fame usually changed back into a cat before entering Billy's trailer park. Suzy broke the silence. "So, we've retrieved Billy's wand, kept Menaus out of doing any kind of magic for a while, and made his wand useless to the other side. What's next?"

"That's easy," said Fame. "Demon hunting." Without another word, she dropped into her cat form.

Suzy took on a dramatic voice as she walked toward Billy's house. "Billy Bobble, Demon Hunter. It sounds like a reality TV show."

Billy followed behind her. "With his trusty sidekick, Suzy Q."

"Why do I have to be the sidekick?"

"Because I have the cool name."

"Really? Bobble-Head is cool?"

"No, but Billy Bobble would be cool if I had my own TV show."

Suzy had to give him that. "Okay, fine. But I'm not a sidekick. I'm an equal partner."

"I stand corrected," said Billy.

Neither of them noticed that Fame stayed behind, and was joined in the shadows by a certain wise old man with a long white beard. "Wish them luck, young one," said the old one.

"They're going to need more than luck."

"True, but a little luck never hurts."

Epilogue

"**M**R. PRESIDENT, THANK YOU for meeting me on such short notice."

"Anytime, General," said the President of the United States. General Quinofski had been in the Oval Office a few times, but never in a one-on-one and never for a meeting that he asked for. He wasn't sure whether to sit or stand, until the President stepped from behind his desk to indicate a chair. "What can I do for you?"

"It's more what I can do for you, sir," said Quinofski. "I have to jog your memory."

The President was confused. "Did I forget something? An appropriations bill?" He glanced down at his notes. "An anniversary? Suzy's birthday is in the summer, yes?"

General Quinofski marveled at how well the President reminded himself of Suzy's name and birthday without appearing to have just read it that second. "No, sir. It's actually the biggest thing that's happened in your — or, any other administration, I'd bet. And I have a feeling that our secret is about to get out, so we'll need to get ahead of it."

"Really? And how did I forget about something so big?"

"In a word? Magic." Before the President could react, General Quinofski said, "Kids."

Suddenly, Billy and Suzy, both nicely dressed for the occasion, appeared in the Oval Office, sitting on the couch opposite Suzy's Dad.

"Good afternoon, Mr. President," said Suzy.

"Nice to see you again, sir," said Billy.

The President's jaw hung nearly to his knees. He looked to the General, then the kids. Without saying a word, he pressed a button on the phone next to him. "Sarah, cancel everything for the rest of the afternoon."

"Yes, sir," said a woman's voice on the other end.

"General, start from the beginning."

R.S. Mellette

ACKNOWLEDGEMENTS

When it comes to Billy and Suzy being in print, the biggest thank you must always go to Matt Sinclair. Where else could I find an editor and publisher who would let me say, "Intelligent design!? You're friggin' kidding me!" in a kid's book? The man is a literary rock star, and I'm not the only author who thinks so.

Kirbi Fagan is next. Her art for this series has always been spot on, and she's a fantastic Facebook friend. Seriously, go friend-request her right now. Her smile will make you happy all day.

After the cover art is done, it's up to a cover designer to put it all together. Charlee Hoffman, thank you so much for that!

R.C. Lewis, who did the book design (that's all of the inside stuff) for *Billy Bobble Makes A Magic Wand*, couldn't squeeze us into her schedule this time because she's too busy being a big successful author with her books *Stitching Snow* and *Spinning Starlight* to help us little people ... (I am so kidding). But she did help Matt-of-all-trades with the nitty gritty details of design. For that I know I'm grateful, and I bet Matt is, too.

Mary Serbe proved that not all writers know what they are doing when it comes to commas, grammar, splitting infinitives, etc. She did the proofreading, so all of you critics who think a possible comma splice ruins an entire book … get over it. Mary did a great job.

Barbara, of course. This year has been full of ups and downs. I don't think I could have gotten through the downs, nor enjoyed the ups, without you. You're a great partner. Thank you.

Matt's family also deserve a big thanks for their loaning him to this project. I couldn't have done it without him, and he couldn't do it without you.

And, finally, thank you for reading!